DOWN the HALLS
and
INTO the STREET

A Novel
by

Linda Parrish

Published by Indigo Arts Press

Published by Indigo Arts Press
First published in paperback by Indigo Arts Press, 2013

ISBN-13: 978-0615754475
ISBN-10: 0615754473

PROLOGUE

HOW YERBA BUENA GOT ITS NAME

The old brujo lowered himself onto his blanket and faced the setting sun. The kinsmen gathered themselves around him, sitting on the hard, bare earth above the rocky shoreline, and waited in silence. One crouched to build a fire from the dry brush and sticks that lay everywhere on the sloping brown hillsides. The wind blew in sharp gusts from the northwest, and the men pulled their robes of skins closer around their shoulders for warmth. The brujo spoke suddenly into the darkening twilight air.

"Here I see a great gathering of the tribes."

The others looked to the west, out beyond the vast, dark waters – more waters than any had ever seen but had only heard of in legend – out to where a strange, misty smoke poured like horse's milk into the many small valleys below. The sun

1

glowed blood-red then fell into the far reaches of the endless waters. They saw the barren sand dunes below them, the black rocks and yellow weeds of the seashore where the water rose in great mounds and then broke against the land. They saw the faint, rolling outlines of dark hills to the south. They saw a wall of misty smoke blowing in from the north. All these things they could see, but they saw no great gathering of men. Such was the power of the old man, that his visions flew beyond this sunset to see a time unknown and a people unknowable.

"I see white mountains, built by men and raised to the sky," the old man said. And he lifted his arms toward the south. "Many white mountains, their peaks in the mists, but shining and glittering from within, even on the blackest of nights." The others looked at each other and at the brujo. How could men build mountains where there was only gray sand and low hills and cold, rocky shores? And how could mountains shine from within, with no sun and no moon to light them? Could men live inside these mountains and could the glittering be from their cooking fires? Or did the old one speak of magic?

"Ancient One," a young man spoke. "How is this strange new land of white mountains called?"

The seer slowly moved his eyes over the land, so different from the hot, dry earth of his home so many days to the southeast. The group had come to see for themselves this great sea of water and to bring the story of it back to their people. *Now that I have seen it,* the old man thought, *I can die in my homeland and be with my ancestors there.*

He brought his deerhide smoking-mixture pouch from under his robes and gestured for the men to fill a pipe and smoke. One by one, their young, smooth faces and their lined, aged faces were lit by the flare of the burning stick as the pipe went from mouth to mouth. The brujo's eyes were closed to small slits and their black depths glinted sharply, reflecting the flaring of the flames, as he watched the darkness descend and the stars appear high above.

He saw other men than these – pale-skinned men with yellow hair and red hair and curled hair and pale eyes, the color of the morning sky, and beards on their faces, and he saw them smoking the pipe under the white mountains. And what they smoked was the good herb, the herb which made them into men of peace. He saw then, with eyes turned inward, that there would be conflict and warring in the new land between the men who built the mountains and the herb-smokers who only wanted to live in brotherhood. This vision saddened and wearied him. Would men never stop warring?

He grew tired. The cold cut through his garments and he longed for the warmth of food and sleep. He raised himself slowly from the ground and stretched the visions out of his muscles, and he saw clearly the men around him once again.

The wind died down then and into the stillness the old man spoke once more.

"This place will be filled with the smoke from the good herb – as much as the cold smoke which flows in from the endless waters on this night."

He turned. The men gazed at him in respectful silence, waiting for his words.

"And therefore the land shall be called Yerba Buena."

The kinsmen gathered their blankets, turned to look at the hills and the sea once more, then made their way back to the camping place and sleep. And the youngest of them carried the pipe and smoking mixture of the eldest.

1 A LONG TIME COMING

She: "What are you rebelling against?"
He: "What've you got?"

The Wild One

The crashers came in through the window. Scrambling, grabbing, giggling up the fire escape and tumbling onto the bare wood floor in the middle of the night. This place might just be alright. It had all the makings for a base of operations, an empty movie set, a place to call home, as in, "Say, Baby – you wanna come home with me?", an address to fill out on an application for public assistance – aid to the totally disabled. "Yesss, I'm totally disabled. Can't tell fantasy from reality. All messed up from the war, the generation gap, Wall Street and Madison Avenue, TV and movies, hardass parents, uptight teachers, the government, the church – what've you got?" It was a whistle stop between destinations, or departures, or points of view – point A to point B in a decade-long trip. No electricity. No hot water. No furniture. But hey – no rent! So they sneaked in while the sneaking was good, while that cigar-chomping, shiny-suited rich bastard they knew the landlord must certainly be had his back turned, while the last tenants were out the door and the new ones had yet to pay their money down. While they were young and healthy enough to jump right back out the window if it came to that. While they had nothing, absolutely nothing, to lose. It was the launch pad for Operation Mind Bend, Project Fuck Authority, from which these untrained and unlicensed pilots would hurl, unaided by spacewalking umbilical cords or Instant Tang. It was the community within the community, the wildlife sanctuary for endangered humans, misfits who fit right in, the Palace Theater, the Big Time. It was a place to get in out of the bastard freezing fog.

It was a much-modified, shored-up and time-forgotten three-storey apartment building squeezed tightly between two others just like it, each with its Victorian old-west facade along the street-facing edge of the roof and its chipped stone stoop and its graybrownish paint job right down to the bubblegum and oil-stain sidewalk. The daylight between the buildings.....well, there was no daylight between the buildings. Where one left off and the other began was a simple matter of a paper-thin wall through which you could hear the muffly noises of the neighbors drunkenly brawling, hacking their cigarette coughs, flushing their toilets, slamming their doors, playing their TV's and having bed-squeaking, wall-thumping sex.

In the manner of shabby apartment buildings everywhere in the City, it was a roach-infested, slumlord-neglected, earthquake-compacted and twisted, tall and skinny construction from another time entirely. Inside, the threadbare, musty carpet ran up long flights of stairs and down long railroad-flat halls and the walls were held together with decaying wood under thick, drab paint. Inside the wooden skeleton was a termite hotel and frayed-wire tangle, dead bug parts commingling with twitching live wood-eaters in every intersection and joint – all that California redwood hauled from the mountains on railroad cars, up Market Street in big wagons by sweating mules and sweating laborers, only to wet-rot down into a black pulp inside the black walls decades later – all that remained of trees that once were so tall they disappeared into cold wild Pacific clouds.

Once there had been real fires of coal in the fireplaces, but they had long ago been boarded over with plywood, now the mantlepiece and hearth were like a beautiful and dramatic curtain closed on a stage that would never again light up the room. Once a team of hairy-handed craftsmen spent long hours carving and polishing the woodwork and wainscoting, framing every wall, decorating the long halls and staircases. Once cherubs chased each other around the molding of the small rooms. The banisters up and down the hundreds of stairs were smooth and turned and ornate. The once-rococo, delicate frivolities of the Victorian school had been unceremoniously raped by Black and Decker power tools, and the flowers and angels lay flattened and buried under decades of dense, leaden paint.

The rooms were miniature and many, and the building divided and subdivided by landlords seeking to squeeze yet one more family into the allotted space, to ring yet one more reluctant greenback out of their long-suffering tenants.

Bathrooms were down the hall, across the way, anywhere but attached to the bedrooms, and even these were divided into smaller units. The toilet had its own tiny compartment – just room enough to sit down and look up at the tall chimney of a ceiling above. The light was a naked bulb with a pull chain. The window was small, crooked and cracked. Next door was a slightly-less-tiny room with a cast-iron bathtub and a sink. Also with the same description of window, which was always simultaneously cracked open and painted shut, always whistling with cold wind and overlooking the light well with three or four battered aluminum garbage cans at the bottom. The view, through the cracked glass and chicken wire, was of other bedrooms and bathrooms and kitchens and a square of gray sky crisscrossed by thick, black frayed utility wires. The bathtub was narrow and deep, short and chipped and cold. The fixtures were the fat porcelain kind that should have been stolen and saved, because now they go for heavy money at the local designer bed-and-bath showroom. The "hot" was on the "cold" side and vice versa, or both knobs said "cold" – a prediction which often came true. The toilet lid had a gigantic crack running down its middle and threatened to divide in two at every flush. The chrome fixtures, mismatching the pedestal sink, blended perfectly with the hideous linoleum, circa 1940, peeling off the floor.

The thrifty landlord had long ago installed a tiny water heater to serve each unit. He found them at a salvage yard, where they wound up after outliving their usefulness. These microscopic appliances could always be counted on to produce a few cupfuls of tepid water per day. Just where they were located was never discovered, so the temperature could never be turned up. The dead of summer in San Francisco could pass for the dead of winter anywhere else, and the only source of heat for the ten rooms in this flat was a skinny wall heater near the kitchen. So the shivering bather, after leaping, blue-skinned, for the ankle-deep clawfoot tub, would have to run down the hall wrapped in a thin, scratchy and wet-from-the-last-bather towel to stand with chattering teeth in front of this heater while hurriedly pulling on stiff jeans and a holey t-shirt. This roaring furnace was permanently turned to the maximum temperature setting in order to keep the immediate vicinity –

say, six inches in either direction – a toasty fifty degrees. Fahrenheit.

The kitchen was like the drab and bare "Honeymooners" set: a single porcelain sink hanging off the wall, chipped to the cast iron and dripped on by a rusty faucet; a gas stove, long past its prime, encrusted with grease and propped crookedly against one wall; an old wooden table with wobbly legs and an assortment of castoff dinette chairs. Nothing else. No counters. No work space. No fridge included – someone brought in an old, round one the size of a depression-era radio, which held two eggs and a bottle of ketchup. The doorless freezer held a six-ounce can of frozen orange juice, always leaking its syrupy contents onto the glacier of neglected frost encasing the compartment. Lives had been risked getting this fridge up the stairs. Huge chunks were ripped out of banisters and walls every time a piece of furniture had to go in or out of a room. Strong men in their prime had to fortify themselves with Miller High Life and a couple of tokes of Columbian before attempting the scaling of the staircase to the third-floor flat. There were always tense moments as couches reached the landing and had to be maneuvered around, over and through spaces made for the dollhouse furniture of a bygone era. Visions of crushed stairs, ripped carpet and gaping holes in the freshly-painted walls sprang to every mind – of smashed rib cages and amputated fingers, of gasping kitchen appliances lying in a heap of twisted metal at the bottom landing, of gasping loved ones lying pinned beneath them, of the landlord's wrath and the amount of dope that would have to be dealt in order to set things straight. Vows were solemnly made to never leave once the furniture was finally in.

The night before the crashers were kicked out by the landlord to make room for paying tenants, Karen from Bakersfield took a lit joint, a candle and a red crayon, and, standing on the toilet lid, covered the bathroom wall with words that came from a new corner of her mind, and she laughed silently as she wrote:

somewhere a blues bum with sour wine breath is counting his change and grumbling to the bus driver somewhere a society matron patron of the arts steps from her gleaming sedan into the neon of her favorite nightspot

somewhere two darkskinned girls are experimenting on each other

somewhere a bank official with a wife and three kids and a diatribe against perversion is trying to decide which dress to wear

somewhere the cityscape is being photographed by a dewy-eyed dreamer

somewhere a streetcar leans over the edge of a Market Street hole

somewhere a sailor scores a piece of ass

somewhere a liquor store is being held up by a pair of little boys

somewhere TV saves the day by cutting off a conversation

somewhere the call of the needle has someone crouching in an icy corner

somewhere the fog laps at the edge of the collective mind

somewhere socks are being mended, heads are being bended, money is being lended, babies are being tended and lives are being ended

somewhere fathers are being congratulated,

suspects are being interrogated, lovers are being infatuated, officials are being inaugurated, minorities are being humiliated, exploits are being exaggerated, weaklings are being dominated, tenants are being relocated, chemicals are being activated, riots are being anticipated, shoes are being elevated and navels are being contemplated

speeches are being talked, sidewalks are being walked, doors are being unlocked, punks are being socked, boats are being docked, old ladies are being shocked, horses are being rocked and watches are being hocked

old stuff is being renewed, booze is being brewed, stamps are being glued, defendants are being sued, oil is being crude, leather is being chewed, perverts are being lewd, tomatoes are being stewed, performers are being booed and suckers are being screwed

dealers are being burned, lessons are being learned, guts are being churned, spits are being turned, hard knocks are being earned, hearts and being yearned and suitors are being spurned

crooks are getting caught, pants are getting hot, answers are being sought, iron is being wrought, smack is being shot, squares are smoking pot,

votes are being bought, wars are being FOREVER
fought and goats are being got
breeds are being bred, faces are being fed, lies are
being said, old folks are sick in bed, flies are
dropping dead, bulls are seeing red, lives are being
led and it's only in your head

Two days later the bathroom was painted with
off-white glossy enamel, which covered Karen's
poem forever and gave off fumes almost as long.

This three-storey apartment building, with its
seemingly accidental assortment of levels, divisions
and rooms, its smells of boiling vegetables, Chinese
incense, fresh paint, mildew, cold metal, streetcar
grease, ocean fog, stale pot smoke and patchouli
oil, and its uninvited guests sleeping like dogs on
its hard floors, had its roots, however shallow, in
the soil of a San Francisco district mapped off and
designated as Haight-Ashbury.

2 DOWN THE HALLS AND INTO THE STREET

Soon as three o'clock rolls around
You finally lay your burden down
Close up your books, get outta your seat
Down the halls and into the street

School Days
Chuck Berry

The freeways leading into California from the East Coast, the Midwest and the South joined up to freeways leading into the San Francisco Bay Area and funneled down onto the Bay Bridge, the Bloody Bayshore and the majestic, fog-shrouded Golden Gate. That summer of 1967, every onramp was full of hitchhikers with their dogs and backpacks and guitars, thumbing their way to this new, wild place called The Haight. Some were running *away* from Mom and Dad and stifling suburban conformity, but most were running *to* what they'd heard was the countercultural center of the Universe, a Mecca for the outcasts they had become in their own home towns and in their own families.

Karen from Bakersfield – a dusty, hot town in the San Juaquin Valley – slipped out the back door of her parents' stucco tract house one morning and caught a ride in the back of a pickup full of sacks of feed. She was later joined by Roger from Tucson, Arizona. They shared a joint Roger had gotten as a parting gift from his older brother and talked about their plans to find a place to live in San Francisco. Heading west at the same time were Dave and Jeff from Iowa, who would later meet up with Karen and Roger in the soup line in the Panhandle of Golden Gate Park.

Buddy Bloom had been living in North Beach, in a tiny bedroom in an apartment he shared with three art students, one of whom smoked sticky black opium all night in a ratty Japanese kimono and played classical music so loud it drove Buddy out into the windy Grant Avenue night. Here it smelled of sweet Italian pastries and espresso from the corner cafes, red wine and pipe smoke from the coffeehouses and bars, wet streets and electric sparks from the roaring buses, and incense, garlic and ginger from the Chinatown tenements just a few blocks away. The darkened mysterious windows of the neighborhood delis were filled with hard salamis in their moldy paper wrappings, fat Chianti bottles with straw-wrapped bottoms, olive oils from Mediterranean slopes, cheeses and biscotti and boxes of dried pasta, and every size and shape of bread, from baguettes to rounded sourdough loaves, hard and soft and in between.

The streets were full of down-and-out hipsters, huddled in cigarette-butt doorways, looking for hot cider and cool jazz, old women in thin old coats and wool headscarves pulling wire shopping carts full of laundry, tourists gaping at the marquees on Broadway where girlie-show barkers promised them a night of topless thrills, bikers in black leather and their peroxide-blonde chicks, Chinese office workers turning up their collars as they got off the streetcar, straight-arrows and punks, hookers and schoolmarms, jazz musicians, homeless winos, night workers, starving artists and every other kind of shadowy face, hidden by the nighttime city.

Buddy loved North Beach, but he had heard about the new generation of rebels coming up behind the beats – getting to be known as "Hippies" – who were crowding the streets of the Haight-Ashbury, and one day he caught a bus to see for himself what it was all about.

He wound up wandering the streets for weeks, up and down Haight between Masonic and Stanyan – five long blocks of the best show in town – looking for a place to relocate and for someone to relocate with. He made the rounds of the neighborhood's trash cans every day, collecting glass bottles to turn in for the refund. On a good day he could make enough to by a plate of fried rice at the Chinese restaurant or a big newspaper full of fish and chips at the Foghorn, where the line inched past five-gallon tins of edible tallow stacked in the hallway – the fat used in the huge fryers. If not, he could always get a plate of watery stew from the Diggers, a group of guys who went around the city collecting discarded or poorly-watched boxes of food from the alleys behind supermarkets and restaurants, later handing it out for free in the Panhandle to anyone who stood in line.

Dave and Jeff were brothers, aged eighteen and seventeen, who had left their widowed mother and one-horse town for the California sun, the California music scene and the California girls. They had been standing on the corner of Haight and Cole when Buddy walked up to them and asked if they knew of any vacant apartments. Before they could answer, Buddy spied some activity over their shoulders that looked like furniture going out of a building and into a van.

"Hold up," he said. "This looks like somebody's moving out of this place right now."

They moved a few steps closer to get a better view. There were three or four guys loading a couch into the back of a van. An elderly woman hugging a sweater around her bony shoulders stood on the stoop, frowning first at the men and the truck, then behind her at the open apartment door. She moved painfully down the steps and a middle-aged man in a suit took her arm and led her to a sedan parked at the curb. Buddy looked up to the top floor of the building and saw there were no curtains in the windows.

"Looks like that third floor is being vacated, Kids. Let's wait around and see."

The three loitered a while, smoking cigarettes and eyeballing the passing girls in their short skirts and tight jeans. Buddy asked the boys where they were from and what they planned to do in the Haight.

"Gotta get jobs," said Dave. "I just graduated, but Jeffy here dropped out – thinks he's not going back, anyway." He punched Jeff lightly on the shoulder, grinning. Then he glanced around uncertainly. "We'll find *some*thin'," he said.

"Yeah," said Jeff. "Even just pumpin' gas or somethin'. *Any*thing, as long as we're doin' it *here.* I ain't never seen anything *like* this place, man!"

"Well, hey," said Buddy, "you can help me pick bottles for a while, and they serve free food in the park. And if that place is gonna stay vacant tonight, we can crash there." He nodded in the direction of the apartment across the street.

"How we gonna get in?" said Jeff. "Hey, man,

I've been climbing fire escapes since back on the old block in Brooklyn!" Buddy said. He laughed and flipped his cigarette butt into the gutter. "Why don't you guys meet me back here at about nine. If the place looks empty, I'll find a way in."

The boys eagerly agreed, then made their way across Haight and down Cole to the park. Buddy stood a while, and when a girl with long, brown hair and big, brown eyes strolled by, he ran his fingers through his hair and fell in step behind her.

Later that night Buddy met up with Dave and Jeff and their new friends, Roger and Karen. Buddy was pleasantly surprised to see there was now a pretty young girl in the mix. She had the look of a small-town teenybopper ready for adventure and enlightenment, and he was just the older-and-wiser San Franciscan for the job. He shot Roger a sidelong glance. Was this guy her boyfriend? No comparison, thought Buddy. Karen wouldn't be able to resist him.

The five of them stood under the fire escape, trying to figure out how to pull it down. Finally

Roger volunteered to lift Karen on his shoulders to reach it. It was a stretch, but she caught the metal bar and pulled as hard as she could, while all four of the guys standing under her gazed, grinning, up her skirt at her day-of-the-week panties.

Buddy led the way and they all climbed, nervously giggling, past the first and second-floor windows. At the top of the fire escape they tried to open the window, but it had been painted shut. Pocket knives were pulled out and every crack was explored. While Buddy and Roger struggled to push the window up, Karen leaned over and tested the other window. To her amazement, it moved.

"Hey you guys," she whispered, "check this out!"

Dave pushed the window the rest of the way and climbed over the railing and window sill, landing with a thump on the floor.

"Far out!" he laughed.

Everyone shushed him at once.

"After you....." said Buddy, as he helped Karen through the window.

Soon the five of them were brushing themselves off and standing in the middle of the dark, bare living room.

"Shhhhh....." said Karen. "The people downstairs might hear us."

"Let's see what's here," Jeff whispered, and tiptoed into the hall.

Buddy pulled his lighter out of his vest pocket and held the flame above his head. They all slowly spread out into the other rooms, stifling laughter and bumping into each other, until Karen and Roger discovered a mattress on the floor in one of the bedrooms. It would have to be the only place for all five of them to sleep tonight.

Buddy slowly felt his way down the long flight of stairs to the front door. He unlocked it and it swung open.

"Hey, guys!" he whispered loudly.

They all crowded onto the top landing.

"I'm going for some food.   Anyone wanna come?"

They all started down the stairs in a clump.

"Wait a minute," said Buddy, "someone's gotta stay here to let us back in."

Dave and Roger agreed to stay and went back up the stairs and into the room with the mattress to have a smoke. As Karen, Buddy and Jeff hurried out the door, Dave and Roger talked about what it had been like hitchhiking west. Dave and his brother had caught a ride with two old rednecks in a dusty Chevy who drove them halfway across Nevada, then left them in a gas station bathroom in the middle of the desert. After a hungry night, their next ride was with kids their own age, driving to California from New England. They all sat around a small campfire they made in the sand off the side of the road and looked at the vast Milky Way stretching across the black silhouettes of mountains, breathed in the dry sage aroma of the still-cooling sands, and talked in soft voices about what they would do once they hit the streets of San Francisco. The driver, Jim, crouched with his genitals hanging out the bottom of his cutoff Levi's, but the rotgut red wine they were passing around made it just not matter.

"I hear there's thousands of hippies livin' there – I saw pictures of `em in Life Magazine," he said. "At least nobody's gonna think *I'm* crazy any more when I'm walkin' down the street with all *them*."

"Fuckin' A!" said a short kid with tattoos on the backs of his hands. "My old lady nearly had me locked up, just `cause I let my hair grow a little bit.....just because I skipped school once or twice. Man, I got outta there just in time!"

A thin 16-year-old girl with lanky blonde hair and lots of jangling jewelry looked at the kids around her and took her first, shy drink of wine. She got dizzy and happy and crawled into a dirty sleeping bag in the back of the car with her boyfriend of five days.

They drove off in the morning, and made it into San Francisco just as the sun was going down behind the Golden Gate in an ocean of pink fog.

When Buddy and the rest got back with the food, they all huddled on the mattress and ate, wiping their hands on their jeans and jackets. Someone had brought some candles and they lit them and stood them up on the floor, where they dripped wax and made dancing shadows on the high ceiling. They talked and laughed for a while, staring at the candle flames, then lay down and drifted off to sleep, hugging each other for warmth, with Karen right in the middle.

Buddy woke up a few hours later to find all the others snoring around him, and slowly crept quietly off the mattress and onto the floor, where he crouched and stared at Karen's dark form, sleeping between Roger and Jeff. As he stared, she sensed his presence and stirred, lifting her head like a deer at a water hole to stare back.

"What's going on?" she whispered.

He put his finger to his lips and motioned for her to follow him. She looked at Roger and the other guys, sleeping like the dead, and quietly disengaged herself from the group and sneaked across the floor to follow Buddy, who had gone out the door and down the hall. He tiptoed through the kitchen, with her following just behind, asking, "Where we going?"

He didn't answer, but opened the door leading off the back of the kitchen to a small, enclosed porch above the back yard, three floors down. She hadn't seen this room before and leaned across Buddy's arm to peer into the dark. He quickly slid his arm around her waist and turned her toward him, pressing his mouth on hers roughly before she had a chance to react. She turned her head to the side, so that his kiss fell on her shoulder, and she pushed him away as hard as she could. He looked at her in frustration.

"C'mon, Karen.....you're so beautiful.....I can make you feel really *good,*" he whispered.

He moved his hand down her hips and quickly up under her skirt, letting out a sigh. She stiffened, pushing him back, then twisting out of his grasp and running out the door and down the hall to the bedroom. He watched her with frustration and anger, shrugging his clothes into place then running a shaky hand through his hair and walking slowly to the landing at the top of the stairs. He paused to see if there were any voices coming from the bedroom, but he heard nothing. Then he sped down the long flight of stairs, out the front door and into the night to catch a bus back to North Beach.

3 FLOWERS IN YOUR HAIR

All across the nation such a strange vibration
People in motion
There's a whole generation with a new explanation
People in motion people in motion

San Francisco
Scott McKenzie

Tom walked into work one morning in the spring of 1967, climbed onto his chair, placed one foot on top of his desk, unzipped his fly and took a leak all over his 'IN' box, his 'OUT' box and his cheap pen set the company had given him in gratitude for ten years of loyal service. With a middle-finger salute to the big cheese himself, who stood gaping in the doorway, he walked out of nine-to-five employment forever. He was thirty.

    Tom had plans. He had plans not to make any plans. He had money in the bank; the day before he had sold the boat he'd been building – the albatross he'd poured all his time, money and energy into for the past four years. His wife,

Sheela, called the boat his Wooden Mistress, grumbling under her breath, "I wish he'd spend half the time caressing me as he does that goddam boat!"

He'd driven down to the warehouse every night after work and run the heavy sanders along its underbelly until his arms went numb, he'd inhaled fiberglass dust and epoxy fumes until his lungs backed up into his throat. He'd sat on the unfinished deck with wood scraps, cans of putty, bags of nails, power tools and snaking cords all around him, smoked a cigarette and asked himself questions.

"Do I really wanna take off into the middle of the Pacific Ocean with Sheela and the kids and maybe land on some desert island and live off coconuts? What are the kids gonna do without TV and ice cream and roller skates? Is Sheela really gonna be happy without her mom and dad and her sisters and her friends? Or is she just goin' along with my pipedream trip, hoping I'll grow out of it and she'll be off the hook? What would everybody say if I just sold the damn thing and quit my fuckin' job and went for a walk in the park?"

He asked Sheela later, "What the hell do I need a job for, anyway?"

Sheela shrugged and glanced pointedly at the three children sleeping in the tiny back room of their trailer.

"I mean," Tom went on, "where is it written you gotta get up at exactly seven-thirty every morning, Monday through Friday, and put on this suit, this *uniform,* and this little piece of cloth around your neck, this *leash,* and get out on the freeway with every other jerk and kill yourself in traffic, getting ulcers.....ya know?"

Sheela knew.

"Then," he said, squinting through the smoke as he took a drag on his Marlboro and hitching up his jeans, "then you gotta sit at some plastic desk all day.....it's not even real *wood,* for cryin' out loud, and you gotta move all these pieces of paper from one little box to another little box, then back again, and pretend to be working, *pretend* to be happy to make the boss man richer than he already *is!*"

He shifted his weight. "You don't even have to *have* a job, ya know. You can just live off the land. There's all kinds of places – California's an empty state. The whole fuckin' state is *bare.* Everybody's crammed like sardines into the Bay Area and L.A. and Sacramento, and the rest is just mountains and redwood trees and creeks. You can build a cabin, grow your own food, fish in a lake. You get up when it's light, go to bed when it's dark. There's no Saturday or Sunday, when everybody's supposed to get out the barbeque grill and eat hamburgers and wear Bermuda shorts, just like everybody else....."

"That's the thing," said Sheela – "we're not just like everybody else, fortunately, so why should we even try to be?"

"And you don't have to punch a time clock and report to some self-important, petty-official *boss* and pretend to be busy so you won't get fired," Tom went on. "Christ, we all live in fear, every moment of the day, of getting *fired.* They hold it over your heads to keep you in line until you ain't doin' your job anymore to, like, *do your job.....*you're just doin' it to keep from getting *fired."*

Sheela smiled at Tom sadly and wiped her red, soapy hands slowly on a towel.

"Why don't you just quit, then, if you hate it so much?"

Tom shifted his weight again, scratched his chin a
bit and took another drag on his cigarette.

"Yeah," he said softly.

The park he took a walk in was Golden Gate. He wasn't thinking, I'm looking for something, for someone, and I know it must be around here somewhere.....But that something was in the air. It was in the wind that blew white fog in fast motion through the tops of the waving, sharp-scented Eucalyptus trees lining the park's walkways. It was under the cold sand or on the slides and swings in the playground and on the sidewalks of Haight Street. It was in the dark doorways and down basement steps and up in musty railroad flats on every block. It was on day-glo black-light posters from Winterland and the Fillmore Auditorium which were thumbtacked and stapled to every telephone pole. It was in the steamy coffeehouses on cold nights, where hot cider with a cinnamon stick was served on cable-spool tables and you could listen to young troubadours sing folk songs until closing time. It was behind lopsided, stained American flags that hung in the bay windows of the old Victorians. It was on the secondhand couches and threadbare Oriental rugs in the tenement apartments up and down every street. It was in cars and pickups and buses bouncing down Oak Street to the freeway crossroads. It was rolled in Zig Zag wheat straw papers and ground in gelatin capsules and smoked and swallowed on Hippie Hill. It was in the music that echoed from every car radio, every nighttime smoky living room and every street corner gathering of longhairs with guitars and harmonicas. It was sitting under a tree, reading a book, and it had long, blonde hair.

Tom's German Shepherd, Scruffy, trotted right over to Carla and put his nose in her face. Laughing, Tom sat down next to her and introduced himself. They exchanged a few words, like people do when they first meet by chance in a park, then Tom strolled off with Scruffy, a little less resolved, somehow, in his plan to make no plans, and Carla went back to her book, a little less able to concentrate on it.

She was reading a passage entitled "Earthquake Weather". "It is an atmospheric condition, most frequently occurring in the late spring or early fall (Indian Summer) in Northern California, characterized by warmer-than-average temperatures, higher-than-average humidity and a yellow-gray, overcast sky. Earthquake weather is further characterized by one or more episodes of momentary and profound stillness. Those who notice these sudden "pauses" describe them as a quick change in the background or ambient noise and air pressure, a sudden tone in the ear, a missed beat in the environment. These seem like moments when no bird sings, no horn honks, no schoolkid yells and the very air gets caught against some invisible logjam in the stream and backs up into one's head like a plug. It is during these pregnant pauses that there is a fleeting but certain premonition of impending events on the magnitude of a devastating earthquake, an atomic explosion – even the Second Coming."

Carla glanced up to see Tom's retreating back and Scruffy's tail swishing high in the still, yellow-gray air.

Carla and Patrick lived in an old Coca-Cola delivery van parked on Fell Street. She spent her days walking up and down the Panhandle, along Haight between Masonic and Stanyan, into the park to listen to the drums on Hippie Hill. It was down from Stanyan, past the pond and under the bridge – she could hear the conga drumbeats rising and falling on the wind as she approached. There were always drummers there, lined up along the flaking green park benches, beating on the tight skin, accompanied by spoons tapping against wine jugs, tambourines, cowbells, blocks, recorders, flutes and clapping hands.

Young girls danced barefoot on the grass in front of the crowd, tie-dyed scarves blowing like flames, unencumbered breasts swaying to the delight of all onlookers. In a kind of Duncanesque ecstasy they twirled alone, no longer needing a partner or a diagram of dance steps. Alice, who had been the cringing wallflower at her school prom, was now grinding her pelvis at eye-level with sweating Black and Chicano and Jewish-hippie drummers, all of them beaming and nodding their enthusiastic approval. Cindy, who was shy to the point of neurosis a few short months ago, danced braless in her see-through Indian cotton dress, eyes closed and arms open. They could do here what they would certainly have been chastised for, might even have been arrested for, at home. Dancing. Alone. In public. Braless. Expressing themselves through movement.

Criminals.

At a given moment, when worn-out hands began needing a rest, the drumming would tangle up and fade out and everyone would have a laugh and the bottle of rotgut wine would be passed around. Joints would come out of inner pockets and secret, inlaid boxes, and matches would be struck on the back seats of tight Levis. A skinny, crumpled reefer would make its way from mouth to mouth until someone intercepted the last quarter-inch, the roach, and stored it away for future use. A boy wearing fringed leather pulled a tiny pouch from the recesses of a grimy velvet vest and carefully tucked the roach away. He had a collection going, and when he had enough for a whole joint, he'd roll the sticky concoction in a fresh Zig Zag and float away on the concentrated high some considered to be superior to fresh.

Soon someone with heavy eyelids and an unwipable smile would try another rhythm and it would be taken up, bit by bit, rising in volume into the wild, windy sky above.

Carla was back at the Coke truck when Patrick came home from his warehouse job every day. They had bought the delivery van on Market Street, in one of those corner lots with six musty-smelling lemons and a salesman with pants so shiny you could see your reflection in them. It was a steal, he assured them, for $250. It was a hippie RV, the only home they could afford. They took out the passenger seat and used the space for a food box. In it they stocked the essentials: Skippy peanut butter. Saltines. Twinkies. Snickers. They lined the back with old carpet and painted the whole thing, inside and out, with swirls and flowers and paisleys and slogans, such as "Custer Died for Your Sins" and "No Hope Without Dope".

Nights were spent huddled warmly inside the truck in a cloud of smoke. The windows steamed up and dripped down. The truck rocked with every car whizzing by on the street. Carla put up paisley Indian bedspreads from Cost Plus in the windows to give them privacy from the swooping headlights. Patrick played his guitar and they harmonized on songs by Woody Guthrie, Bob Dylan, Ian Tyson and Tom Paxton.

They slept soundly, cuddled in sleeping bags zipped together. They had it all because they had each other.

Tiny, rock-hard acorns, clay-like manure the

park gardeners spread to fertilize the grass, and sand laced with broken bottles made the barefoot walk a perilous one on those foggy summer mornings. The early risers would wipe condensation from the windows of their buses and vans, pull on cold jeans and wait for the slow-moving park attendant to open the bathrooms. These kids had given up warm beds, hot showers and a fridge full of food in cozy suburban homes for thin, beat-up sleeping bags in the back of trucks and outdoor bathrooms with cold, wet grit covering the concrete floors. The toilet seats were usually missing, as were the doors to the stalls, and one had to bring one's own toilet paper, since the only paper in sight was soaking up fetid black water on the floor.

It was difficult, even then, to find a gas station with unlocked bathrooms. Comfort stations were for paying customers, not jobless, unwashed longhairs. The invasion of the street hippies proved to be the last straw, and the doors of public facilities everywhere were slammed shut by crewcutted, jumpsuited station managers who spat in contempt at the thought of a hippie ass touching the toilet seat they'd just cleaned with Lysol. The message was clear:

"Get a job, a house, a *haircut* and a car to buy gas for, you pinko, peacenik, dirty hippie commie scum!"

God-fearing America wasn't ready for this army of barefoot flower sniffers to contaminate what had always been the sacred domain of the greenback-carrying motorist. Everyone knew freaks did not go into bathrooms to simply relieve themselves in the normal manner. They went in there to deface, masturbate, shoot up, have homosexual encounters and leave vile, contagious diseases on the seat.

San Francisco, famous from its birth as a melting pot of cultures and for its tolerance toward deviant lifestyles, began an unofficial war: Straight versus Hip. One of the first front lines formed at the now-locked doors of gas-station restrooms. It was the same war-of-attrition thinking that was behind the law against feeding pigeons – the idea being that if old folks on the part benches and little kids on playgrounds didn't feed the city's thousands of pigeons they would surely all die of starvation and people wouldn't have to look at the shit on window ledges. The idea behind denying bathroomless people access to toilets was that they'd be forced to *go somewhere else*, preferably to another country. But, as the urine-saturated stairwells and feces-covered vacant lots of every major city in America will attest, it didn't work. And San Francisco has more pigeons than ever.

Tom went home to Sheela and the kids the night he first saw Carla. Carla and Patrick went to the Chinese restaurant up the street to share a huge, eighty-five-cent plate of fried rice. Carla somehow wound up back under the tree in the park the next afternoon, and Tom somehow found himself walking toward her with a crooked smile on his face. Before the day was over, they were strolling down the melted-chewing-gum and broken-glass sidewalk, staring into headshop windows, eating candy bars, listening to pavement performances by hippies with guitars and tin cans, talking to strangers, holding hands and laughing at everything and nothing. They were sharing a secret, and nothing is more delicious than the unspoken, telepathic knowledge of a love about to happen.

For a moment, as they stood staring at a flock of birds take off from the rooftops, all sounds paused, they felt something plug up their ears, and as they turned to look at each other the wild fog parted and the sun burst out, and with it, a rainbow.

4 SHE'S LEAVING HOME

One of these days I'm gonna stop my listening
Gonna raise my head up high
One of these days I'm gonna raise my glistening
wings and fly

Society's Child
Janis Ian

Your sons and your daughters are beyond your
command

The Times They Are A-Changin'
Bob Dylan

Carla stepped out of the suburbs. Like the tragic heroine of that sad and inspired Lennon/McCartney song, she was making her getaway from the tracts and everything they had come to represent. The pink, blue, green or yellow pastel stucco house from which a three-piece-suited businessman would emerge every morning at 8:30 sharp, leaving behind a wife in fuzzy slippers and hair rollers and three freckled, blonde kids eating Cheerios and watching cartoons. The American-made gas-guzzler in the driveway, polished to a high gloss for the five-minute trip to the supermarket. The TV dinner, served on a TV tray, in front of the TV set, with its hot-on-the-top, frozen-on-the-bottom assortment of tasteless and carcinogen-ridden chow – a heartbreaking letdown after an early childhood of home cooking. The sparkle-stucco ceiling, from which every possible erotic picture had long since been wrested during those restless teenage nights. Dragging the main in a hot rod with a blasting radio, that mindless yet essential activity, the object of which was to be seen by as many envious girls, lustful boys and outraged adults as possible in the course of one burger-and-fries Saturday night. Typing and shorthand, which you had to opt for in school because all girls stared out in "real" life as efficient and neatly-groomed secretaries until they landed a husband, preferably The Boss, after which their job was to stop learning and start cooking, cleaning and having kids (it wouldn't do for a girl to get too much education, to surpass her mom's I.Q. or to want more from life than marriage and motherhood). Paying room and board to your parents, who, until the day you turned eighteen, had at least been willing to house and feed you. A generation gap like the Grand Canyon, with the kids on one side, unwilling to even acknowledge anything that happened before their first pimple, and the fretful, angry parents on the other, still trying to squeeze the round pegs that were their offspring into the square holes of their own ideas and upbringing.

"Where did we fail?" was born as kids invented new ways to reject anything not directly connected with rock and roll. Mom and Dad had fully expected to give birth to carbon copies of themselves (forgetting somehow that they weren't copies of their own parents) – duplicates which could be easily molded into more businessmen and housewives, reflecting and perpetuating their every character trait, rising to their exact level of intellect and financial status, rooting for the same team, drinking the same brand of beer, marrying in the same church and giving birth to three more copies shortly thereafter.

Martini consumption skyrocketed, Miltown

prescriptions doubled as horrified parents were forced to watch their kids grow up overnight into total strangers, not even remotely cute or freckled, no longer the spit and image of their old man and devoted mom, growing their hair long, wearing intentionally-ragged clothes, barely speaking the same language, entertaining themselves in ways never dreamed of, listening to music beyond their elders' ability to comprehend or appreciate and laughing in the face of power, social standing, money, religion, respectability, the flag and apple pie. Why, in God's name, did this have to happen *here?*

Carla's great, great, etc. grandfather came across the plains pulling a handcart, bringing his worldly possessions to a land flowing with milk and honey, hoping to settle down with his wives and kids where the neighbors wouldn't be inclined to tar and feather them. Salt Lake City, Utah – the Promised Land. Where men were men and women were chattel. And they were all built like brick shithouses. Big bones. Big, wide hips and great big breasts for birthing and feeding the multitudes of children it was their duty to bear.

Carla was no exception. She had all-American pioneer blood flowing in her veins. But to the everlasting dismay of her parents, who had no backup plan for dealing with kids with independent minds, she could never quite *be* all-American. She could never quite rally behind the school team, the prom, the beehive hairdo, going to college for the purpose of finding a man, Tupperware parties in the den, bridge parties on the patio, three kids in bunkbeds, serving the perfect cocktail to the husband's boss or shaving her armpits. While her classmates attended the senior prom in floor-length taffeta gowns and rented tuxedos, twisting and shouting to surf music, she went drinking with her pals and watching foreign movies at the art cinema. While other girls were pressing corsages into heavy books and mooning, starry-eyed, over their first goodnight kiss, Carla was rolling in the wet park grass and singing Dylan songs with a bloodstream full of vodka stolen from someone's dad's wet bar. While promises were being whispered of engagement rings and job offers, Carla and her friends were smoking corncob pipes in the downtown alleys and talking with street bums about life in the gutter.

And Carla waited impatiently for that magic ticket to All Things – the high school diploma – before making an unceremonious exit with empty pockets and a "you'll-come-crawling-back" look from her mother. She opened the front door, picked up her little suitcase in one hand and her portable stereo record player in the other, and walked out, breaking into a run as she approached the waiting car parked down the block, where her mom couldn't see. But her mom was sitting on the living room floor, in front of the TV, with dry eyes and her mouth set in a line.

It was July 4, 1966. Independence Day.

Nic was waiting for her with the motor running. His own suitcase and a couple of sleeping bags were in the back. They were going to B.C., to live in his aunt's little house overlooking a lake in the green northern woods. Like Stingo and Sophie, they were running away together to the farm – the simple, idyllic existence, where life progressed from love to marriage to children in an organic, natural way, and not as the result of a list of rules nailed to the door.

And like Stingo, Nic, in his pure heart, was saving his dreamgirl from sadness and pain and captivity, spiriting her away to the life she deserved, the life he knew he could give her. That was his quest – and for the moment, it seemed to be within his grasp.

But, like Sophie, Carla hadn't *really* made her final choice yet, but only dreamed she had, sometime on that final night.

Nic had first noticed Carla in history class. She had seemed aloof and untouchable and seemed to possess a secret about the world which he wanted to know. She was different. She wore moccasins instead of pointy-toed heels. Her hair was long and natural, not a mile high with spray. Her legs were unshaved. She wore a plain skirt and black turtleneck sweater. He stared at her.

When she caught him, he shook his head, blushing, and told her she was getting worse every day. She rolled her eyes, dismissing him as being one more conservative adversary judging her, and went to her seat. Why couldn't everyone just leave her alone? Wasn't it enough that her parents and teachers, all adults, in fact, with the possible exception of her art teacher, who looked like Dagwood Bumstead but was as much of a hipster as a public schoolteacher could get away with at the time – they were unanimous in their condemnation of nonconformity, and never missed an opportunity to tell her so, but now she also had to take it from her own peers?

One day Nic approached her, still blushing, and asked for her phone number. Just like that.

"I thought you said I was getting worse every day," she said, with a little lift of her eyebrows. "Why would you want to go out with *me?*"

She held up her hand, waiting for an answer. He pushed his Buddy Holly glasses up on his nose, shifted his weight to the other foot, tilted his head to the other side and looked at her helplessly.

Carla suddenly saw why he had been so interested in how she looked and dressed. And how he had been kidding both of them with his comments.   She looked more closely at his Scandanavian-blonde hair and his flushed, embarrassed face, his awkward stance by his desk, his long, freckled fingers clutching his books in front of his jacket. She took a piece of paper from his desk, wrote her phone number on it, and handed it to him with what she hoped was a penetrating look. He finally managed a small grin, while the blood rushed in his veins.

They went to a movie. He spent the whole time trying to put his arm around her shoulders without her noticing. She spent the whole time pretending not to notice, although her senses were so heightened by the vibrations surging between them she would have felt a microbe touch her.

When he asked to kiss her goodnight, she nodded with downcast eyes. She wound up kissing him back. There was something inexpressibly sweet in his silent, innocent longing. At the tender age of eighteen, she had been suddenly elevated to the role of older-and-more-experienced woman, the one destined to introduce him to love, when she barely knew of it herself.

For the next two weeks, he drove to the dark end of her street every night, and waited for her to come to him. They hid in the depths of the car, under the moving shadows of the leafy trees, and kissed each other into the night. One such evening, when the delicious warmth became too much, Nic willingly and hopelessly surrendered his virginity to her. Then, taking her onto his lap, he kissed her over and over, telling her everything he felt for her in French, hiding inside a language he thought she would not understand, in order to be able to say it. Carla pretended not to understand his words, although she understood enough of both his words and his feelings. She was overwhelmed, disbelieving, undeserving, guilty for her inability to return his intensity, immobilized by indecision – and she never wanted him to stop.

They made plans. The first was to leave for Canada, his home, right after school was out, to drive through California, Oregon and Washington, to break free from everything here and start a new life together. He talked to her for hours in his quiet, far-away voice about how beautiful it was going to be and how much she would learn to love his home, once she saw it, and hoping she would learn to love *him*, once she allowed herself to know him.   But Carla was heartlessly and mindlessly soaking in his love for *her*. She didn't know how to return it. Some part of her knew it was wrong to take without giving back, but she was like a junkie, just wanting another fix of the best drug in the world.

Now, as they sped up the freeway toward that fantasy life, they turned up the radio, rolled down the windows and laughed,

"Goodbye USA! Hello Canada!"

They slept on the cold beaches at night, zipping the sleeping bags together and clinging to each other – the only two in the world for those full-moon-bathed hours on the freezing Pacific sands. They made a fire, they ate something out of a can, they had no water and went thirsty all night, but they held tight to each other's young bodies until the gray light came up in the morning.

Nic's mind was turning over and over with

visions of their lives together, maybe even their marriage, maybe even their children. He looked at Carla again and again, half expecting her to disappear from the seat beside him. Carla watched the mountains and the evergreens stream by the open window, both afraid and thrilled to be free, but safe, completely safe, with Nic. She couldn't understand the depth of her affect on him, couldn't see herself through his eyes. His willingness to take care of her was a mystery which bordered on an uneasy, guilty feeling – the burden of having made him happy without really knowing how she did it, as though it were not her, but someone else, he was seeing when he looked at her. She wasn't trained or prepared for his simple kindness, was too young to know how to respond to him. She understood conditional love, but not the other kind. She wondered if she deserved him.

As they pulled into the Canadian border station, the guards leaned in the window, asking Nic all the usual questions, checking his I.D. and giving him the go-ahead. But they asked Carla how much money she had, and they didn't like the answer, which was, "None".

They asked her to step out of the car and into that little room, sat her down in a chair and interrogated her like a suspect in a criminal investigation. They asked if she was running away from home, and she replied, "No, I'm walking." They said she had to be twenty-one to be considered an adult in Canada. She said it was 18 in the U.S. – something they must have already known. They asked if she was pregnant – evidently the only plausible reason they could think of for a girl to leave home. She said, "It's none of your business." They looked at each other and advised her to turn around and go home to Mom and Dad. She didn't. She turned around and went back to the car where Nic waited, a dark cloud over his head. When she told him they wouldn't let her across the border, both their hearts sank.

This changed everything.

They had to figure out what to do. Slowly and despondently, they drove the streets of the little border town, looking for a motel where they could at least stay the night. They found something cheap and checked in, looking at each other across the threadbare little room in silence.

Nic made a decision. He'd go across the border into Vancouver, find Robert, who had gone to Canada a few weeks before, and bring him back. He gave Carla some money for food, then took off as the sun was going down behind the fir trees across the highway.

She stared at the ceiling, watching the lights from passing cars sweep across from one side to the other, unable to sleep, wondering what she would do if she never saw Nic again. She cried, paced the floor and stared out at the parking lot, willing his car to pull in. It seemed days passed this way, and she had never been so alone.

Then suddenly, Nic and Robert appeared at the door, but only Robert was smiling. Carla was amazed. How had Nic found him? By what magical instinct had he gone into this big city and located one scruffy teenage hippie with a guitar from a crowd of thousands? It was superhuman. Carla looked at him with new eyes, but she did it too late.

The three of them spent cold, dark hours struggling with a direction to go, waiting for a decision to burst through their agony. Carla couldn't think. Everything had been turned upside-down. She stared helplessly from one to the other, crying for all three of them. Robert lay on top of the bed with is arm thrown over his eyes, motionless. Nic sat slouched in an armchair, his jacket still on, staring with burning eyes at Carla's white face. She couldn't look at him then. A song was playing in her heart – the saddest music in the world. She didn't write it down until nearly 50 years later.

In the end, it was Nic who released the other two from the weight of decision. He slowly rose from the chair, reached into his jacket pocket for the car keys, and tossed them onto the bed in front of Robert. The three of them went to the door. Carla and Robert followed Nic out to the gravel parking lot in front. He quietly got his things from the back seat, shut the door, and turned to face them.

Carla moved to Nic's side, and gently taking

his arm, led him a few feet away and then stood in front of him. She looked up into his pale blue eyes, forcing herself to keep looking after what she saw there. It would take her many years to finally understand the turning point they had come to in this moment and to comprehend the bottomless pain that comes from wishing you could do it all over again and change *everything*. She leaned up and kissed his mouth, which was cold and unmoving. Then she said simply, "I will *never* forget you."

He memorized Carla's face for a moment, saying nothing, then turned and started walking north.

She watched him slowly recede into the morning fog. She thought this was the bravest thing she had ever seen. What was she losing? What was left behind? His form got smaller and smaller, dissolving into the gray. Then he was gone.

5 AFTER LIVING ALONE

Where did it go that yester glow
When we could feel the wheel of life turn our way

Yesterme Yesteryou Yesterday
Stevie Wonder

Carla and Robert headed back south the next day. Having a vague idea about somehow winding up in New York City, center of all things hip and wild, they zigzagged around the northwest a while longer, discovering bits and pieces of life after high school as they went. And they unearthed one all-important truth they'd always suspected, though their parents had done their best to convince them otherwise: *They were not alone.*

In their junior year they had taken a Saturday trip to San Francisco – fifty miles away, but a foreign country. The City had atmosphere. The City was not the `burbs. They got off the cable car, which cost a quarter and never had a waiting line, in North Beach and laughed their way down Mason

Street, looking at doorknobs. Bob swore Mason Street had the best doorknobs anywhere. Rusted, blackened, chipped, painted, crooked and timeworn, they each bore a long history of being grasped by human hands and rubbed slowly away by their touch.

They looked in all the coffeehouses and Italian restaurants and bakeries, at the old men on benches in the park in front of the big stone church, at the bookstore windows and narrow alleyways between storefronts and apartment buildings. Tall, windy canyons where black shapes crouched like monsters. Naked, dim bulbs throwing yellow light onto bricks and peeling doors. Steamvents blowing blue clouds up and over the walls. They had espresso in tiny white cups at a sidewalk cafe and wondered about what went on at Finocchio's – where men actually dressed up like women in sequined gowns and feather boas, putting on shows, pantomiming, batting inch-long false lashes at the crowd. *Why would a man do that?* Were they *queer?* What did it *mean?*

Carla had heard the word enough – in dirty

jokes told by her father and his poker-playing buddies, late on Saturday nights, through the walls. She had to use her imagination, since no direct information was ever provided, as to precisely what homosexuality was all about. The message from all directions was short and to the point: It was too twisted and sick to even *think* about. Do *not* think about it. The concept will infect your brain like a mass of worms and leave you fatally corrupted in some dark way you're too young to understand. A friend in school had made the remark one day at lunchtime that Johnny Mathis was a "queer", excusing himself to Carla for even uttering the word. From then on Carla was unable to listen to one of his phenomenally-beautiful songs without picturing him singing it to a boyfriend. It was a surreal image, indeed. Both her parents would have died on the spot if they had known their youngest child, the baby of the family, blonde-haired, blue-eyed, beautiful Diane, was a lesbian to the core, and that Carla could have gone either way.

They rode the bus from downtown, up Market Street, sitting next to a hippie woman before hippies had a label – a post-beat, pre-Berkeley student radical missing link, whose running monologue forewarned them:

"Don't listen to any of the happy horseshit they're gonna hand you.....all this political stuff and keep off the grass and have a church wedding," as she chewed on an enormous wad of bubble gum, looking more than a little equine herself. "Do whatever's groovy, ya know? And don't let them hand you any horseshit." She leaned closer. "*You have a right to be free!*" And then leaned back, nodding knowingly, until the bus swung up Haight Street where she got off, her long, wild hair blending right in with the scenery.

"What the *hell?*" said Carla.

They had just rolled into a whole new world. As the bus alternately flew at breakneck speed and screeched to passenger-killing halts toward the park, Carla and Robert stared out the window at a sidewalk full of men with long hair. *Very* long hair. Hair down the middle of their backs. Ponytailed hair. Braided hair. Headbanded hair. *Beribboned* hair. As bumpkins from Suburbia High, Carla and Robert had been told that a guy's hair was too long if it touched the tops of his ears or brushed the back of his ivy-league, button-down collar, and Carla's mother went berserk if her daughter's bangs came anywhere near her eyes. She demanded that Carla keep them cut short or she'd do it for her. She asked, in a near-rage of incredulity, if Carla intended to have long hair when she was *twenty-five years old?!* (As it turned out, Carla did. And the dire consequences her mother, speaking for conformist society in general, had predicted did not come to pass as a result. On the contrary, it was the height of fashion at the time.) The dean of boys had loved nothing better than to yell at Robert to *get a haircut!* every time they happened to pass in the halls. The dean of boys and his ilk seemed to believe, because they *wished* it were true, that there was an actual, physiological difference between the growth potentials of male and female hair. Robert was pleasantly shocked when, after a few months abstinence from the barber, his hair actually got longer!

The length of one's hair became an issue of monumental proportion, with extreme prejudice and reaction on both sides. There was nothing like a flattop to label a guy a square or a hawk or a narc, or maybe all three, and nothing like long locks to let the world know you were a pothead, commie peacenik. The streets were full of squares who came in to gawk in fascination at the longhairs, but somehow never the other way around. Straights hated hippies with an unreasoning passion, yet they couldn't take their eyes off them, especially the braless girls. The tour bus company even had a special run up Haight Street, just so tourists from all over the country could feign shock when they saw live hippies, like so many zoo animals, with their own eyes. For some reason never really examined or explained (and this will sound familiar to the gay/lesbian community), long hair was a threat to decency, morality, patriotism, cleanliness and righteousness – the very American Dream we'd come to revere – as though virtue of any kind and long strands of hair could not possibly occupy the same space at the same time.

The blinders were coming off. Carla and Robert had proof that they just couldn't be the craziest kids alive, because there before their eyes, on the streets of the Haight-Ashbury, deviance and free expression of every kind (except the violent, hateful kind) raged completely unchecked. Good will was let loose from its cage and was spreading brotherly love in every direction..

Run for your lives.

One extreme gave way to the next as they made the return trip to the South Bay via the Southern Pacific commuter train. They sat in the back of the coach and giggled at the row upon row of businessmen clones, each in an identical suit-and-tie ensemble, each with his briefcase and umbrella, each with his precisely-quartered Wall Street Journal, which he left on the seat at Belmont or Palo Alto.

The kids got home, flipped on the stereo and stared up at the sparkle-cottage-cheese ceiling while the answer, my friend, blew in the wind. There was something smothering them to death in the pastel houses with their cardboard-thin walls and flimsy doors which didn't begin to keep out the sound of the TV every night or the arguing and yelling from the poker games on weekends, and didn't keep *in* their music, private talks or secret plans.

Sometimes Carla felt as though she were looking at herself from a distance as she went through the motions of living this life which had been assigned to her. Sharing a room with her sister because her parents could never afford a fourth bedroom and didn't believe children needed or deserved privacy. Lawrence Welk, the anti-rocker, every Sunday night and boxing every Wednesday and soap operas and inane sitcoms and game shows during the day. Fixing dinner for her parents and their friends while they were out golfing, then cleaning the kitchen afterward while they played cards. Wearing the cheap, embarrassing clothes her mother picked out for her, even wearing her hair according to her mother's long-outmoded and painfully-embarrassing tastes.

The kids were even forced to go to church once in a while, where Carla learned before she even had words for it that there was no true faith behind all this churchgoing, that it was an attempt to keep up appearances in front of the neighbors and other church members, and this made her hate it even more. There seemed to be two kinds of Mormons: Good Mormons who attended every meeting (and there were a *lot* of meetings), paid ten percent of their income to the church, earned their way into a temple wedding, got baptized for the dead and threw open their doors to the ward teachers who always showed up at dinnertime – and Jack Mormons, like Carla's family, who lived on the periphery of the religion, keeping just enough of a foot in the door to make sure the Relief Society would someday cater their funerals.

Everyone in Carla's family groaned when the ward teachers came around just as they were sitting down to Salisbury steak on TV trays in front of "Bonanza" – most of all Carla's dad, who would be compelled to stub out his Winston and hide the beer can or coffee mug. These missionaries, plodding on the treadmill of Good Works, were inevitably ancient and slow and had the personalities of retired morticians. They had gray hair and pale, damp skin with red patches. They wore dark blue suits and cheap, shiny ties. They smelled like a combination of terminal illness and their wives' bath salts. They had soft, phlegm-clogged voices and spoke as though every word was being pulled from a bottomless well of memories by ancient tortoises. They'd make themselves at home on the plastic-covered couch and spend about forty-five minutes talking about fishing with Dad while the kids squirmed like the captive animals they in fact were. Then, as if remembering suddenly why they had walked into the room, they would read a little fairy tale from the Bible or the Book of Mormon and say a little prayer for the Brothers and the Sisters. When the door finally closed behind them, Carla and her siblings could only secretly roll their eyes at each other and stifle miserable laughter.

Carla's religious guilt was based not on sinful activity, but on sinful thought. While she was still young and gullible enough to believe in an omniscient deity, she felt certain her thoughts alone were sufficient to sentence her to Hell. And she was encouraged in this by everyone from her parents to her teachers to her fellow students, who constantly pointed out her differences and her failure to fit in, and warned her against any deep speculation regarding religion. She was expected to believe that The Lord works in mysterious ways and that mere mortals had neither the capacity to comprehend his will nor the right to question it. And yet, at the same time, she was also expected to believe that *certain* mortals understood God's mysterious ways perfectly, and that it was *their* duty to tell you what God wanted you to do, or else. Everything from drinking coffee to murdering your neighbor was a no-no, but questioning religion had a special place in Hell, just for Carla. She asked the Sunday-school teacher, after a lesson on unconditional faith,

"If God wants us to have blind faith.....why did he give us eyes?"

The teacher slammed her copy of the New Testament down on the table and stared at Carla, infuriated. Controlling her voice with difficulty, she ordered Carla out of the room and down to the bishop's office to meet her punishment – a grim lecture and a phone call to her parents.

Though she rolled her pleated skirts and

ratted and sprayed her hair into the near-perfect flip, she lacked genuine enthusiasm for becoming the virginal, cheerleading, dictation-taking Sandra Dee she was evidently expected to be. She had no group. She didn't belong with the honor-roll squares in plaid blouses and winged glasses, but she didn't have the nerve to be bad and smoke cigarettes with the crowd at the Dairy Belle, either. She couldn't relate to most of the girls and had no idea what to say to boys.

Standing in line at the cafeteria one day, inhaling the humid aroma of creamed corn and boiled hot dogs, she happened to notice Jim Keller – a wild, black-jacketed James Dean type most girls were afraid to even make eye contact with. He was slouched along the wall with his buddies, combing his oily hair and cooly eyeballing the line, when a girl with large breasts and an illegal amount of black eyeliner came bouncing up to him, put her hand on his arm and whispered something in his ear. He gave her a slow smirk, then actually burst out laughing! Carla was silently and deeply mortified. This kind of ability – to go up to a guy, *touch* him, then whisper in his ear and make it interesting and clever enough to actually make him *laugh* – this was simply beyond her comprehension. Who *was* this girl? How did she get so comfortable with guys that she knew how to get their attention and make jokes with them? Carla felt at that moment that she would never reach that level of sophistication, not if she lived to be a thousand. Her whole life to that point seemed to be compressed into an insignificant, ineffectual handful of days. She was invisible.

Carla was saved by her looks. Not much else mattered in high school. Boys were attracted to her blonde hair, pretty, girl-next-door face and early-onset ripeness in the breast department. Voluptuous yet chaste. Intellectually, she was ahead of her time but, thankfully, too introverted to join in the debate. What more could a teenage boy with a bloodstream full of testosterone ask? Monroe and Mansfield were images to aspire to: enormous breasts, blonde hair, juicy lips – these were guaranteed to get you a man. Then putting it all away once you got him, staying in the Formica kitchen and cooking dinner and pressing his shirts and keeping your opinions to yourself – these

74

would *keep* him.

She went out with a surfer guy in white Levi's whose only goal was to get her into the sack. As soon as he did, he dumped her for being too easy to get into the sack. She went out with the best-looking, most shallow guy in school, then wound up liking his best friend more – an average-looking guy with a sardonic wit and a fabulous kissing technique. She went out with a neurotic Italian baseball player who wanted to marry her and have lots and lots of kids (an idea which had zero appeal to her at the time). Then she went out with the older brother of one of her art-class buddies, who took her to a drive-in movie and kissed her blind, then dumped her because she was, don't you know, too *hard* to get into the sack.

Robert wore a navy peacoat and a peace button and combat boots to school, and the dean didn't know what to do with him. His father was a swarthy Eastern-European brute who once tried to strangle him while Carla sat between them in the car. He carried a beat-up guitar, wore a corduroy cap, and fancied himself to be a kind of combination Bob Dylan/Woody Guthrie down-and-outer who had ridden the rails everywhere and seen everything. Carla was attracted to him because he didn't fit in any more than she did.

Sallie and Carla started hanging out together when they discovered a mutual interest in folk music, the peace movement and an unconventional style of dress. Sallie had lots of sisters and no father and a mother with the smallest feet Carla had ever seen on an adult woman. When she saw a pair of high-heeled mules next to Sallie's mom's bed one day, she thought they belonged to a doll. The family kept a parakeet that drank root beer and said "Gimme a break!", and a little black dog that slept at the foot of Sallie's bed. Carla would go over to her house after school, sometimes with Robert, and they'd play records and talk about what they would do once they got out of suburbia.

Sallie somehow managed to get tickets to the Bob Dylan concert at the civic auditorium, which she lost for a few days then found after frantically tearing the house apart. They were in the freezer. The three of them went together. Robert joined the rest of the crowd of acoustic-folk-music purists who walked out when Dylan brought out his electric guitar and his band for the second half of the show, but Sallie and Carla couldn't have been crowbarred out of their seats. Carla was completely overwhelmed, madly in love, moved to tears by this skinny little poet with the messiest hair in the world. She was astonished, her mouth hanging open, at his ability to flawlessly execute two hours worth of songs without using notes, to nail every situation and concept with perfect, boggling lyrics, to read her mind, to play a shiny black grand piano, to say what he had to say, seemingly uninvolved in showmanship or celebrity, then put down his guitar and walk off, no encores. This was, for Carla, the essence of cool and the epitome of art. *Why,* she screamed silently, was she still stuck in *high school*, still stuck at home with her *parents*, when meanwhile *real life* was taking place, *elsewhere, without her?* What she had just seen had done nothing less than change her life forever.

Carla and Robert had tried sex a few times out of a sense of inevitability – no one else would have anything to do with either one of them. They had become too deviant in a school full of straight arrows and prom queens. It was awkward, even ridiculous, and left Carla none the wiser regarding why people were so eager to engage in it. Sallie sensed it without being told, and had her heart broken. She accused Carla of betrayal and cried. Carla didn't know what the hell had just happened, or why.

She and Sallie had talked about guys in general, and had agreed that they were basically dicks, and that they weren't interested in getting romantic with them, although Carla was not a virgin and couldn't keep from trying to find out how sex was *supposed to be.* She didn't see, at the time, how her sexual relationship with anyone else could or should effect her close bond with Sallie, much less break it apart.

Years later, she ran into Sallie and instantly saw what she had been too naïve to see before. Sallie was with a woman, and although Carla was not introduced, she instinctively knew that this was Sallie's lover. She thought back with some sadness to the night when she and Sallie and Robert had been sitting on the couch in Sallie's darkened living room listening to music. Peter, Paul and Mary were singing "Early Mornin' Rain". Robert had his arm around Carla's shoulder and Carla had her arm around what she *thought* was *Sallie's* shoulder. After a long time she suddenly realized it was not her shoulder at all, but her breast. When she quickly moved her hand, Sallie said emphatically,

"It's OK! Nobody's getting hurt!", as if to admonish Carla not to be so hung up about old-fashioned concepts. "Aren't we above all that?" she said. And she took Carla's hand and placed it back where it had been and they went on listening to the next song.

And now as she stood looking at Sallie years later, she wanted to say how sorry she was, how if she had known, if she hadn't been too young, if it had only happened a few years later when Carla realized her own essential bisexuality, things might have gone differently, and how Robert had definitely not been worth it after all. But everyone was uncomfortable and shuffling their feet and Sallie hurried off and Carla never saw her again.

Carla and Robert were now looking for adventure in Washington and Oregon, hitchhiking under perpetually-gray Northwestern skies, not talking about Sallie or Nic or school or the first eighteen years of their lives. They were happy to be young, happy to be on the road, happy to be free.

6 CAN'T HELP BUT WONDER WHERE I'M BOUND

My existence led by confusion boats
Mutiny from stern to bow
Ah, but I was so much older then
I'm younger than that now

My Back Pages
Bob Dylan

They got off the train in Portland with a dog, a bag of biscuits and two Mexican centavos. They asked some passerby if they had landed in a college town, and after being directed to Portland State, headed off through the sunny streets and green, leafy park. They struck up a conversation with a guy who lived in a cave dug from the side of a berry-vine-covered hill, and he invited them to spend the night. Having few alternatives, they followed him through the thorny bushes to his hideaway that night, and stood shivering while he went ahead to inspect the small cave for signs of possible breaking and entering. To this hobo, who never gave the same name twice, but who called himself Ranger that night, every face on the street was the face of a potential enemy out to steal him blind, turn him in, uncover his secrets and generally undo his meticulous, fugitive M.O.

He lit the stump of a candle and crawled into the tiny opening, silently inspecting the mysterious interior for what seemed like hours before he gave them the all-clear to come in. There was barely room for the three of them to lie down, and the only source of light – the broken candle – disclosed the hobo's pitiful collection of belongings: a few boxes containing an arcane assortment of drug-related paraphernalia, which he apparently guarded with his life, an orange crate where he set the candle and an old, torn sleeping bag. Carla couldn't even guess what he ate or how he took care of the basic functions of life.

As they huddled together and stared at the shadows on the damp walls in front of them, the fugitive pulled out limp pouches and plastic bags, matches and an ancient pipe made of well-rubbed stone. He pinched small crumbs between his fingers and shaped and reshaped them to fit the tiny pipe bowl. When he finally had the hashish in place, he went on to the protracted ritual of folding the remaining hash in a bit of foil, tucking that away into a plastic baggie, placing the baggie in a flaking leather pouch and, after several glances around him on every side, removing a rock from the floor of the cave and putting the pouch in, covering the whole thing with one of his boxes and leaning up against it in a final, protective gesture.

Carla and Robert looked at each other, sensing they were in the presence of not only great mystery, but great weirdness.

They soon crawled under their damp sleeping bags, which were completely insufficient against the cold and damp of a Pacific Northwest night, even if it was the middle of summer. Carla lay awake until morning, hearing unidentifiable noises all around and fearing wild animals, cops, Ranger's cave robbers, maybe even aliens or monsters from the berry patch.

Back on the park bench the next morning, they tried to make eye contact with student types. Sooner or later, somebody had to feel sorry for them. Kent sat down next to them and immediately offered his place – a small bedroom in an apartment he shared with a "really nice" couple. They spent a few nights sleeping there, in Kent little bed, while he slept on the floor. The couple he roomed with were junkies who floated past Carla's peripheral vision, staring at her with deep suspicion as they crept in and out of the shared bathroom. Carla had no idea why anyone would find her the least bit threatening. She felt the couple being strange and furtive, giving off bad vibes, but she was as yet unaware of the hard-drug world and the paranoia which was its hallmark.

Robert went off every morning to see if he could find casual labor. One such day Kent asked Carla to have sex with him. So this was the deal, she thought. He expected it as a payment for the place to stay. She couldn't have been less tempted or less attracted to him. He was nondescript, dirty, poor and more than a little strange and hard to read. He smoked his own custom blend of herbs and weeds because he was too afraid of the law to possess or smoke pot. He seemed to subsist on money he got selling bits of junk he found in garbage cans and alleyways, and shopped exclusively at the Salvation Army thrift store. While Kent was trying to convince Carla to go to bed with him, she was trying to figure out how to explain her revulsion not only towards him, but towards the idea of selling herself in exchange for a room – without offending him too overtly. She wasn't self-confident enough, not yet, to just tell him to fuck off.

As they sat side-by-side on the bed, which was the only place to sit in the room, Robert came back, threw open the door, and saw them there. His mind, which always worked overtime under normal circumstances, leaped at lightspeed to the conclusion that they were already deep in some torrid affair behind his back, and he threw an unchecked tantrum, as though he had actually found them in the act. He accused her of every description of infidelity, ironically ignorant of the fact she had been engaged in saying no to that very thing when he came in. He wouldn't have cared if he had known, only seeing what he chose to in order to justify his actions to himself, if no one else.

He ran out the door in a fit of heavy,

sickening theatrics. She followed him up and down the sidewalk, both terrified and furious at the same time at the idea that she was now his possession and was no longer allowed to speak to members of the opposite sex. She hadn't signed up for this.

Robert broke away and ran back into the house, crashing into the shower with all his clothes on and breaking a glass shampoo bottle for emphasis. He came out with one of his hands bleeding from a small cut, and started sobbing. Carla, unable to stand such violence, such psychotic emotion, was forced into the position of apologizer and peacemaker. Using tactics she wished she didn't possess, almost didn't know she did until that moment, she told him what he wanted to hear in order to get him back to a normal, manageable state.

"Robert, *listen to me.* We weren't doing *anything*, I swear to *God.* He was just showing me some pictures."

And she pointed to the small photo album at the end of the bed. Robert glanced up at her with hatred.

"Jesus!" she said. "I *do not* want to go to bed with him, period!"

She looked at Kent, who stood impassively by the window, smoking.

Shaking her head, she went on, "I'm your girlfriend, OK? And you're my boyfriend." She felt sick at her own words, but went on. "I'm not gonna sleep with other guys, OK? Can you just accept that? Can I have a *conversation* with a guy without you flipping out like this?"

He looked up and didn't say anything, but at least he'd stopped crying. She sighed and held her head in her hands. Fucking *men!* she thought. And not for the last time.

"Look," she said, "why don't we just go find another place to stay, if you're so upset. I don't like it here, anyway." She shot a glance at Kent, who turned away and went to the kitchen.

At this, Robert looked up and smiled a little. Oh my God!, thought Carla.   He's just like a goddamn *kid!* The hairs on the back of her neck were standing up and she felt a knot of anxiety in her belly as she realized that now she was going to be walking on eggshells, watching everything she said or did, for fear he might find some hidden meaning in it and go completely insane.

Were *all* men like this?   She had always been terrified of her father.   He was big and had a strong smell and loomed over her when she was small and fragile.   He had a hair-trigger temper.   His normal speaking voice was just short of a booming yell.   He hit her and her brother and sister with his belt.   He got drunk and nasty.   He gave orders and criticized and bullied everyone and laughed at people who weren't like him. He smoked cigarettes, making the whole house stink, said "God damn it!" a lot, slamming his hand down for emphasis, making his two little girls jump in fright.   Riding in the back seat of the family car with him was always a white-knuckle experience.   He would allow no other car to remain in front of him for long, but passed them all, routinely hitting eighty or ninety miles an hour and waiting until the last possible second before pulling back into his own lane. He sat in front of the TV every weekend, watching sports, with a beer in one hand and a cigarette in the other and yelling at the screen because they weren't playing the game the way *he* would play it. Carla promised herself at a very young age she would never marry a man even remotely like her father.

She wondered now, watching Robert wipe his eyes and brighten at the thought that he owned her and could tell her what to do, if there were men out there somewhere who were *not like this*, and if so, why didn't they come to her rescue?

It would take her several decades to finally realize that when it came to romantic love, males and females seemed to be not only working from different definitions, but reading from different dictionaries.

Yes, to dance beneath the diamond sky with one hand waving free
Silhouetted by the sea, circled by the circus sands
With all memory and fate driven deep beneath the waves
Let me forget about today until tomorrow

Mr. Tambourine Man
Bob Dylan

Sad Eyed Lady of the Lowlands was rolling like honey out of the stereo speakers. Six or seven reclining bodies were planted around the floor on pillows, soaking up the words like sponges, as though there might be a pop quiz later. They stared, open-mouthed, heavy-lidded, at each new verse, looking inward, wondering if there were no end to the epic, unfathomable poetry this guy could come up with, wondering why they had huge lumps in their throats, wondering what the hell he was *really* saying. But it wasn't that. No – it didn't matter if Dylan was just having a laugh, twisting words around in a sleight-of-tongue exercise, making a personal molehill of no consequence into a mountain of esoteric pathos and passing it off as high art. It didn't matter whether Dylan could sing like Caruso or the Beatles were more popular than Jesus. Each person in that room worshiped at the alter of *how it was being said.*

The walls of Jack's room were covered in colored burlap, each wall a different color. Not only did it keep the place toasty against the eternal Portland mist but it gave it an air of Bohemian chic. Jack had his long, white finger on the pulse of all things avant garde, and he stared at his audience and stroked his goatee with deep satisfaction. He placed a fringed scarf over an old floor lamp and the light went down and the bodies slumped a few inches lower. The music came through clear and visceral and hypnotic. Smoke hung in a head-level haze. Eyes met.

They sat in a corner room of a big, old apartment building in collegiate Portland in the summer of 1966. Jack had produced the spectacle of Bob Dylan's newest album with a flourish from his velvet book bag. He had run around to everyone's room, telling them they wouldn't believe their ears.

"It's just too much this time," he said. "The man has outdone himself. You *gotta* hear it. My room. Five minutes."

Then, when all the basement people were ready, when each had positioned himself according to his own version of undivided attention, when the joint was rolled, lit and on its way around the room, Jack tenderly placed the needle in the groove and slowly leaned back with folded arms. He grinned an evil grin with the bursting knowledge that he'd been the first one in the room to hear it – he was the only one with a turntable and money to buy records, after all – that he had single-handedly gone out into the world and discovered this treasure and brought it back with trembling fingers to the waiting fold. Jesus, life was sweet, Jack thought, as he played with the ends of his Fu Manchu mustache. Look at them! God, how they're loving it! And he looked at Carla a little longer than the rest.

Jack was 26. This made him older and wiser.

He had a job, a steady income. He went to school part-time. He knew where to buy grass. He was one of the few hippies in a town that hadn't quite made it past "beatnik". He had books all over his room – books that he had actually read – books on witchcraft and the occult, philosophy and Eastern religion, and when he put on his black velvet cape with the red satin lining, he was transformed into the high priest of hip, ministering to his little flock of devotees.

By day he worked in his father's bookstore, ringing up sales and keeping the shelves stocked. He perched on a stool behind the counter, peering through wire-rimmed glasses into the pages of thick volumes on philosophy and herbal medicine and white magic. A tiny heater kept his feet warm and folk music scratched from the old record player. He drank gallons of Mu tea which he brewed on a hotplate in the back room and sipped out of a Chinese tea cup. The bookstore was musty and smelled of the sandalwood incense burning in an ashy heap on a tin tray by the window. Customers could sit on the dusty old loveseat near the front window and read poetry as long as they liked – it was all the same to Jack. He wanted to be the provider of the experience. He loved having his domain filled with seekers and he loved giving them what they sought.

Now he reached over to take the burning roach from Patrick, giving him a brotherly smile as he did. Dylan was moaning about "your matchbook songs and your gypsy hymns" and Patrick smiled and nodded with airtight knowledge. Patrick was a music man himself. He was just out of the Navy, where, according to his verbal resume, all he'd done was drink. He had lived on the outskirts of Tokyo with a ravishing, brainless Japanese whore. He came back to the states with a gleaming Martin guitar and a taste for rice wrapped in seaweed – a poor man's version of sushi. On the floor next to his mattress he kept a fat black binder full of the lyrics and chords to hundreds of folk songs. He'd sit cross-legged on the bed for hours, drinking rotgut Red Mountain wine and singing ballads of beautiful women and desperate men. And, like the hobos and outlaws in his songs, he was the silent type when it came to his past. A few reluctant words here and there, and he'd shrug and fall silent. All that mattered was here and now.

He looked around through reddened eyes. Kent sat to his left, his arms wrapped around his knees, rocking slightly with the music. Patrick didn't know about Kent. Nobody did. He had his own small cubicle of a room in the basement and smoked his legal weeds and seemed always to be hiding something. Everyone suspected him. Maybe he was a narc. Maybe he was an informer. Or maybe he was just too weird, even in a group of weirdos. He couldn't even get into the club that was made up of people who couldn't get into clubs. He had followed Carla and Robert from the junkies' apartment and rented his room near the communal kitchen, while Carla and Robert shared a slightly-larger room in a far corner. Ron – a blonde, freckled kid from somewhere in the Deep South, leaned against a wall with a jelly jar full of wine and gazed sleepily around the room. Carla lay on her back with her head near one of the speakers, smoking a cigarette and marveling. Robert sat with his arms clutching his knees and his head buried between them.

No one dared speak until the last notes of the song faded out. No one spoke as Jack tiptoed across to the turntable and repositioned the needle to start the song all over again.

Jack's eyes drifted back to Carla again, and his smile faded. She stared at the ceiling and blew smoke rings, but she could feel Jack watching her. And she knew with what emotion he was regarding her. She didn't return his gaze. She knew it would be noticed by the ever-vigilant Robert. Fortunately, he kept his head down and saw nothing. He was just lost in the idea that he could somehow *be* Bob Dylan.

The communal kitchen was tiny and ill-equipped, but nobody did much cooking anyway. Carla, being the only female in the basement, would try to make a few things, like jello and spaghetti and soup from cans. Her cooking skills were limited. She hadn't yet heard about such culinary basics as sauteed vegetables or pasta al dente, since the vegetables she'd eaten at home had been first frozen, then boiled for twenty or thirty minutes, and the only pasta she knew about was criminally-overcooked spaghetti from a can. The first time she tasted steamed, fresh asparagus she couldn't believe it was in fact the same vegetable that came white and limp and mushy out of a can, tasting of sour aluminum. The first time she had real Chinese food at a restaurant in Chinatown, she was astonished at the vast universe of difference between this and the canned chow mien her mother used to bring home from Safeway on special occasions. Monosodium Glutamate and soggy bean sprouts over deep-fried noodles from cans, eaten with forks from plastic plates – this had been Ethnic Night in Suburbia.

Carla had her first and last encounter with Lysergic Acid Diethylamide one cold, clear night in Portland. The whole crowd from the basement apartments had moved into an old, multi-room Victorian which Ken had finessed out of an unsuspecting landlord. Ken was the candy man, the dealer. He had big enamel pans of sugar water soaking kilos of grass all over his room. Stacks of twenty-dollar bills lay on the bed. Bags of pills, capsules, paper tabs of acid were strewn everywhere. What the hell did he care. He made a bundle, was smart enough to stay out of his own supply and moved to L.A., where he is now giving himself a coronary in the record-producing business.

Robert blew in one afternoon, clutching the door frame for support and grasping a capsule of LSD as though it contained the final key to the final mystery. After staring at it in trepidation for a silent while, Robert and Patrick and Carla opened it up and divided the powder into three equal piles, knowing as much about its potential effects as they knew about nuclear physics. Casting their fate to the wind, they got up from the twilight kitchen and ventured out the front door, over which someone had hung a hand-painted sign, "The House of the Rising Sun".

An hour later the three of them were knee-deep in the water of a tiered concrete fountain that splashed in front of a giant office tower in downtown Portland. Fully clothed, they were frolicking like they hadn't done since childhood, playing with the water as though it were some astonishing new substance and only they knew about it. It was this warm, wet stuff that ran through their transparent fingers and tasted sweet and made their t-shirts all sticky. It was liquid brotherly love. It was the tears of the laughter of angels. How had they missed it before? They laughed at just the sight of each other in telepathic bliss. They were in the ultimate secret club. Who *were* all these outsiders – the faceless, unenlightened drones milling around the fountain, afraid to come in? *Why* were they so uptight? Couldn't they *see?* Carla scooped the water and laughed and laughed. It was bliss. Pure and simple. It was ecstasy under the waterfall with a brainpan full of honey-dripping-microscope-heaven-on-earth-spiral-eyes-everything-is-everything   love juice.

But wait a minute. Everything began to sharpen up, like a camera lens going from blurry to focus. It was getting cold, sitting there in those heavy, wet jeans. There was a rolling black cloud overhead. Carla felt her jaw tighten up as her perception did a slow twist. It was like a foreshortened roaring drunk followed by a mental hangover. The lights were too bright and the noises were too loud. She felt that if she sat still she would be smothered by hyper-reality.

The three began walking, bouncing, nearly running to get to a friend's house. One of them remembered how to get there, and they jumped fences and sprinted across a highway and found the stained-glass door.

Carla stared at the bathroom floor. The tiny shards of tile that had been laid there seemed to be a psychedelic mosaic from just a few minutes ago, but she knew the floor was there long before psychedelic was even a word. How could it be? Never mind. They couldn't stay. They had to keep moving.

They blazed a trail of electric energy into town and back to the house as the hours of the night crawled by. Robert and Patrick began hallucinating like fiends, watching a Roman orgy in the surface of a stone wall, pointing out the details with teeth-clenching glee while Carla, seeing nothing but an extremely clear stone wall, begged, "OK, you guys, great, but let's get the hell out of here, alright?" It was desperate energy, right on the edge. She felt she needed to stay one jump ahead of the input that threatened to overwhelm her, looming at her back like a landslide.

The crystal lights danced in the sky above the bridges of the city. Neon and concrete and fog and music coming out of bars and traffic whooshing by. The sweet, sickening smell of the lumber mills overlapped and seeped into everything. And on the flashing streets of downtown everyone became a plainclothes cop. One look into Patrick's round eyes, one look at Robert's lumbering, lurching walk, one glance at Carla's waterhole skittishness and it would be all over. They'd go crazy if they had to spend even a split second in conversation with a serious, sober person wearing a badge. It would be unthinkable, like trying to converse with a member of another species. They'd be instantly, completely and probably permanently busted.

Back at the dark house, Patrick went upstairs to his room and saw a tawny griffin stalk the tall grass of his peripheral vision. Carla gripped the cold porcelain and threw up into the heartless toilet. Robert picked up his guitar but couldn't play. He wept at the beauty of the strings.

Downstairs in the kitchen a visitor had appeared – a friend of a friend who became Carla's reality check, anchor and support person because she was the only one in the house not on drugs.

Out on the streets again, colored lights twinkled from the infinitely mysterious hillsides. What in hell could possibly be going on up there in those terraced mansions, those castles of secret, lush, dripping wealth. Rich people with every hair in place floated in darkened rooms and performed slow, soft, wealthy acts. Acts of faraway mystery and voluptuous zen artistry and intellect which Carla tried to grasp in her swirling, fleeting imagination as they stood on a curb and tried to decide which direction to risk. As the light turned green and they launched themselves into the intersection of some blazing, wet street corner, Carla felt gravity foreshorten her until she became a gnome – an old man with gnarled, bowed legs and perhaps even an endless repertoire of wise sayings, if she could only remember them.....

Patrick laughed, his eyes shining. "I'm so high I forgot how to ride a bicycle!" he said.

Carla got the idea of the game immediately, and came back with her own declaration of stonedness, "I'm so high I agree with my parents!"

Patrick broke out in renewed hysterics while Robert shook his head, smiling broadly. "Oh yeah?" he said. "*I'm* so fucked up I understand the lyrics to *Louie, Louie!*"

Even as they fell over each other with laughter, Carla suddenly noticed they were doing it in the middle of a sidewalk and people were stopping to stare at them. She grabbed their arms and dragged them away, telling them to *please* act *normal*, which only made them laugh harder.

They found their way back to the house one final time after hours and hours of zig-zagging the city sidewalks. The three of them fell onto a bed at last. Closing her eyes, Carla saw slow-motion fireworks, skeletons, carnival shooting galleries full of duckies and bunnies. Sparks of ideas that could save the very world were born and evaporated in infinitely-short moments of genius.

They struggled to sleep. They moaned to each other. Words were painful. They were afraid to be alone. They couldn't get comfortable. They wanted the sun to come up. They wanted to be hungry for breakfast. The perfect irony – they wanted to feel *normal.* It's called coming down, and it lasts forever.

8 YOU DON'T OWN ME

*Well you know that I'm a wicked guy and I was born
with a jealous mind
And I can't spend my whole life tryin' just to make
you toe the line
You better run for your life if you can, little girl
Hide your head in the sand, little girl
I catch you with another man, that's the end, little
girl*

Run For Your Life
The Beatles

*I'm young, and I love to be young
I'm free, and I love to be free
To live my life the way I want
To say and do whatever I please*

You Don't Own Me
Lesley Gore

Word came around that there was a party
somewhere and they all went, no question about it.

Longhairs in black turtlenecks and patched Levi's, Indian jewelry, feathers, felt hats, sandals and boots, satin and velvet and lace skirts and shirts and vests – all crowded into a dim, rickety old Craftsman house on the side of a hill. A group stood clustered on the steps outside, one of them singing in a conspiratorially low voice, "...Father McKenzie, wiping the dirt from his hands as he walks from the grave – no one was saved..." Carla wondered, what dark new music was this? Only the Beatles, going where no rock band had gone before, with *Eleanor Rigby* on their new mysteriously-entitled album, *Revolver.* Red lights inside the Indian-bedspread-draped living room, candles waving and flickering on smiling lips and half-closed eyes, jug wine going around, music blasting, secret, passionate glances between dancers and drinkers, blissful laughter, strange snacks, blacklight posters glowing from the walls.

Jack watched Carla from across the room as she sat listening to Dylan sing the saddest song in the world about Hollis Brown. She blew slow smoke rings and felt tears well up for this tragic story inside the speakers. She felt Jack watching her again and felt a pang of unease mixed with a thrill of recognition. She was up to *here* with men – living with a hoard of them, putting up with their egocentric bullshit, playing mother, sister and imaginary girlfriend to them all. Could there be any way to fit yet one more into her crowded heart?

Oh God, oh God here he comes.....

Jack sat down next to her and began stroking her hand in the most tender and irresistible way, and the wine rushed through her blood. She squirmed inside, twisting and turning the temptation and guilt around like pieces of a puzzle, trying to explain it all to her frowning conscience. She was so young and so ready for a guy just to be *nice* to her. She closed her eyes and saw Nic walking away.

Jack rose slowly and took her by the hand and led her outside and they stood on the porch, not knowing what to say. And somewhere between their first telepathic realization and that tiny magnetic, breathless move toward a secret and delicious kiss, Robert lurched by in his neverending search for trouble and strife, and grasped the entire, lurid scene in a glance.

He threw himself off the porch and onto the street, unleashing a tantrum of unprecedented proportions under the yellow streetlight – Stanley Kowalski minus the astute perception – madly rending his garments in a torment of martyrdom at the hands of the faithless Carla. She somehow mustered the strength to face him. She grabbed his arm and led him down the street, away from the partygoers staring and listening to the spectacle. As they moved out of earshot, away from the streetlamp, into the darkness, away from Jack's sad face, Carla started crying and couldn't stop.

"Robert, this is it!" she said. "I'm not gonna do this anymore. You've gotta let me go! Just give up on me! Let me be this way, let me be the heartless bitch you think I am – because I *AM* that heartless bitch, OK? I don't love you! *I never did.* I'm not ready to be with one guy for the rest of my life. Let me make my own mistakes......I can't stand being watched and followed and mistrusted all the goddamn time! I'm not the one you want......that's for *sure!* Go find someone who's willing to do it your way, but stop trying to own me and stop trying to fucking *change* me!"

Robert said nothing then, but merely thrust his hands deep in his coat pockets, staring at her with pathetic hatred, then whirled and stumbled down the street in bitter dejection.

From that moment, Carla began to scheme with single-minded determination toward Robert's disappearance from her life. He was eating LSD and methamphetamine like salted peanuts, spending the better part of his time too drugged to have a conversation and scaring the shit out of everyone in the house. His personality, his actions, his outbursts were too dark and destructive for even the speed freaks and glue sniffers to relate to. He would sit in front of an open window for days at a time, chain smoking and mumbling and playing his beat-up guitar into the Portland drizzle. No doubt he was hashing out the Cosmic Enigma, but why the hell, Carla asked herself, couldn't he do it *somewhere else?*

He'd speak darkly about how he was going to get himself a shotgun, go down to the river and blow his brains out, in the style of Hemingway. The quintessential suffering artist. The misunderstood, abused young poetic genius, unable to withstand the insensitive rejection of an indifferent world and a godless universe.

"I'm gonna get a shotgun, just like Hemingway," he sneered at Carla. "I'm gonna sit by the river, then I'm gonna stick it in my mouth and pull the trigger!" Then he took a long drag on a crumpled cigarette and blew the smoke out the open window and refused to acknowledge her further. She thought he might just do it. She hoped he would.

One day he just left. He said he was going to New York at last, because that was where all the action was, that was where he would finally find some people who understood him. No one said a word to try and stop him. Carla held her breath as he walked away, afraid he'd change his mind and turn back.

After six months of gray mist coming out of gray skies, of listening to Ken, the dope dealer, and his all-night pals play Love's *Little Red Book* for the ten-thousandth time on the cheap, loud stereo, after school was out and supplies were out and it just looked like more of the same, Carla and Patrick, who fell together almost by default, got pregnant and got married by a justice of the peace at City Hall, packed up their little VW bug and struck out across the snowy Oregon hills for the promised land – a land flowing with raw, unpasteurized milk and organic, unfiltered honey. The corner of Haight and Ashbury, San Francisco, California.

9 THE HAPPENING

And I feel to be a cog in something turning
Well maybe it is just the time of year
Or maybe it's the time of man
I don't know who I am
But you know life is for learning

Woodstock
Joni Mitchell

They made it just in time. Descending from the snow-covered hills of the borderland, crawling down the wet freeways with all their worldly goods piled in the back of the VW bug, they spotted the final and unmistakable landmark leading home – the smoky-blue silhouette of Mount Tamalpais standing guard at the entrance to the home town Carla never, until this moment, knew how much she loved. San Francisco.

Wandering around, asking directions, they made their way to the corner of Haight and Ashbury and parked the car. The January sun peeked through the clouds long enough to illuminate a street filled with longhairs, barefoot and clanging and smoking and singing, headed east and west with guitars slung behind them, laughing with white teeth through baby beards, young and healthy and taking it entirely for granted in the middle of free America!

Patrick looked up into the windows. Out popped two faces who invited them with smiles to come on in and stay for a while. They carted their bags up a flight of stairs into a white Victorian on the most famous corner in the world and stayed for two weeks. They both came down with the flu, but exorcised it by drinking gallons of green Japanese tea and eating moon cakes, having their tea ceremonies around a little fruit-crate table and later doing lots of sweating under the sleeping bags.

The streets were alive in a kind of latter-day gold rush. People milled thick in the hopes that whatever was going on would rub off, that everything worth experiencing could be experienced firsthand – right here, right now. Word was circulating that there was going to be a happening.   The posters flapping from every telephone pole and from the cover of the new countercultural magazine, The Oracle, advertised, in swirling script, an event called a "Gathering of the Tribes", a "Human Be-In".   Carla wondered silently what it was all about, whether she would be admitted to the event, whether it was too hip for her, out of her league.   Patrick had no such misgivings and wouldn't have missed it for anything.

Carla's doubts were wiped away as they hitchhiked into the park and got out near the Polo Fields and saw all around them a literal sea of heads stretching in every direction and converging on some flatbed trucks from which rock music was blasting into the bright winter air.   There on that huge expanse of industrial-strength lawn, which lay perpetually wet and fragrant with manure, were more hippies than anyone had ever known to exist – out of the California woodwork to be counted in that number, to be part of what can only be described as the vast minority.

A gathering of the tribes, indeed.   Every

deviation from the gray-flannel-suit norm was represented here, where hipness hadn't yet been patented, exploited or made to get on its knees to a producer. There were still fresh recruits, young blood, idealists to take up the banner. Carla was only eighteen and for her it was the birth, not the death, of Hippie.

Balloons sailed up and were met by people sailing down at the ends of parachutes. Kites of all colors flew in a stiff breeze, iridescent soap bubbles popped on frizzy hair, smoke and wine fumes snaked into every nostril, music blared into the wind, words were lost then came bouncing back. Bikers swaggered, bare-chested, beer bottles in tattooed hands, chains slung from belt loops, greasy foreheads furrowed as they scanned the crowd of pale, skinny peaceniks for potential faces to bash. Barefoot flower children, fresh from their meditation rooms and reeking of patchouli and sandalwood, floated above the ground, their white garments billowing and their silver jewelry jangling. Beatle-browed mods in velvet flares and embroidered waistcoats gazed down their noses through blue hexagonal glasses. Organic riceheads from Humboldt County and Mendocino and Santa Cruz and the Russian River arrived in buses and vans swirling with Merry-Prankster paint jobs and full of mattresses and pillows, their patchwork kids in tow, and mingled with urban acid freaks, militants, student activists, gays, soldiers on leave, runaways, North Beach beats, priests, rabbis, dropouts and homeless vets and junkies and winos and earth mamas and renaissance men. They swarmed and swayed and milled and danced and tripped.

The appointed heavyweights of the day addressed the multitudes. Tim Leary advised one and all to drop out of junior executive and drop out of senior executive, after having first tuned in and turned on. Allen Ginsberg, Jerry Rubin and others took their turn at the microphone. The Greatful Dead and the Quicksilver Messenger Service played long and loud to the adoring crowd of twenty or thirty thousand – those who had room danced, those who didn't moved in place to the irresistible rhythms.

There was LSD in the sandwiches and

lemonade passed among the unsuspecting mob, and some were happy to be dosed and some were not. Carla was fortunate enough to miss a second acid trip; she was pregnant, nauseated and still fighting off the flu, and passed on the refreshments. She longed for the comfort and quiet of her bed in their little room. Patrick wanted to stay forever, but reluctantly agreed to take her home.

As they walked slowly back toward Haight Street, they were among an overflow from the Be-In that filled the sidewalks, blocked the streets, rearranged the traffic and attracted curious attention with whooping and singing and jumping stonedness. The tourists watched in scandalized outrage, shaking their heads and clucking their tongues.

"Commies! Dirty, lazy bums! Get a haircut! Lookit that one – can't tell whether it's a boy or a girl, haw, haw, haw!"

Flattopped, beer-bellied guys stood and nudged each other, self-righteous in the knowledge that at least everyone could tell which gender *they* were.

Mark the mandala painter grooved with each brush stroke as he sat glued to radio coverage of the event in his monochromatic Midwest house. He would soon join their ranks, find enlightenment with LSD, marry two women and a man, and help found a successful, self-supporting communal farm in the country.

Sarah from Michigan floated down the sidewalk, electrified out of her skull by one of those acid-laced sandwiches, and memorized the next twelve hours as the single most meaningful event of her life. She was hopelessly, madly in love with every face she saw around her, and found herself in a huddled group of people who chanted, eyes closed and arms embracing, until they fell to the floor and slept.

Rick from New York met his old lady there – she proved irresistible in her braless leather minidress and dayglo face paint.

Danny freaked out when the Hell's Angels tried to frisk him, and ran screaming into the eucalyptus trees, visions of Nazis who wanted to castrate him and shave his head chasing him while the Angels laughed and swilled beer. Afterward, he woke up with the realization that he had an inner consciousness which had eluded him the first twenty-seven years of his life and which catapulted him out of a gloomy and soul-crushing accounting job in Oakland.

Ron from Alabama smoked more pot than he had ever done in one sitting, got up, brushed himself off and strolled down the street, swinging his arms and head in slow motion, in time to all the beautiful love songs he'd ever heard, looking deep into the eyes of more heavenly women than he could imagine, one after the other, until he met the green eyes of the most beautiful of them all. He stopped. She stopped. He reached out, infinitely slowly, and tenderly took her hand. The world faded into a blur of soft color around them. Ron turned carefully and started walking, gently pulling the girl with him. They fell into step, side-by-side, gliding along in a soundproof bubble – their own planet. Ron felt his head swell to a giant balloon, filled with cotton candy, singing birds and arrows going through hearts. The girl beside him smiled like a Madonna, flowers burst into bloom in her footsteps, a rainbow crowned her golden hair. They walked for what seemed like an eternity, neither of them saying a single word, until they came to a corner where Ron turned to read in her eyes which way they would go next. She smiled, but her eyes became suddenly nervous and shy. She spoke.

"What are we doing?" she said. Her eyes darted to the left and right.

Ron felt a black cloud cross overhead. His smile vanished. He released her hand and his fell at his side without hope. He gazed at her beautiful young face with profound sadness. Without a word, he turned away and melted into the crowd.

10 HELL, NO!

Ah the wars, they will be fought again
The holy dove, she will be caught again
And bought and sold and bought again
The dove is never free

Anthem
Leonard Cohen

Remember Charlie? Remember Baker?
They left their childhood on every acre
And who was wrong? And who was right?
And did it matter in the thick of the fight?

Good Night, Saigon
Billy Joel

"Dirty commies! You don't like it here, get the hell OUT!"

    "Chickenshit fags! I fought for this country so you could be free! Ungrateful bastards!"

"Go back to Russia, you fucking assholes!"

The shouting, fist-waving men stood behind a line of cops, wearing hardhats and plaid shirts and jeans and workboots, carrying little American flags and shouting with blood-red faces at the demonstrators walking by on Market Street. Most of the peace marchers ignored their shouts, and only held their signs higher and chanted louder. Some yelled back,

"We're Americans, too! We have freedom of speech, and nobody's gonna take it away from us! This war is WRONG! Out of Vietnam NOW! NO MORE WAR! NO MORE WAR!"

Two or three hardhats broke through the police lines and threw themselves at the nearest protesters, grabbing their signs and ripping them to pieces, then going after the marchers, grabbing guys by their jackets and punching them in the face with the kind of fierce hatred usually reserved for child molesters or serial killers. Some fought back, but most backed away, regarding the irony of the spectacle and shaking their heads. The cops, who generally sympathized with the spectators, gave it a few extra seconds before they waded in to break it up. They pulled out their nightsticks and took aim at all heads of long hair, bashing and bloodletting with more than their normal level of enthusiasm and dragging marchers away to the waiting paddy wagons. The press was right there, snapping pictures for the morning's papers, making sure to get the closest shots of the bloodiest heads.

The march flowed on like a river around them.

"HEY, HEY, LBJ – HOW MANY KIDS DID YOU KILL TODAY?" echoed out into the city streets and bounced off the stone walls of the high buildings. The windows were filled with watching office workers, some booing and waving their fists, some cheering and clapping and throwing confetti. Guys stood around an oil-drum fire and, one by one, reached into their wallets, took out their draft cards, held them in the air for the crowd to see, ripped them in half and threw them in. Each flareup was greeted by cheers from the appreciative marchers passing slowly by. The chant was taken up every few minutes: "HELL NO! WE WON'T GO!"

Middle-aged women walked arm-in-arm, carrying signs that said, "You Can't Have My Son!" Mothers with their babies in strollers wore t-shirts which read, "War is Not Healthy for Children and Other Living Things". Groups of student radicals waved their signs: "KILL A COMMIE FOR CHRIST" and "U.S. OUT OF VIETNAM NOW".

Dayglo peace symbols were everywhere, the first amendment was printed on large placards, the air was filled with incense and soap bubbles and singing. Drag queens walked arm-in-arm with dykes, holding a hand-painted banner that read, "Gays and Lesbians for PEACE". Ministers, priests, rabbis, minor politicians, businessmen and celebrities marched beside street people, flower children, Berkeley radicals, Vietnam vets in their wheelchairs, nuns, communists, Buddhists, Jesus freaks, atheists, militants and college professors. Groups draped in white sheets carried cardboard coffins and held signs listing the latest body count. Huge blowups of newspaper headlines and pictures of bloodied Vietnamese women and children dotted the parade. A wagon carried a styrofoam Statue of Liberty with an army-issue rifle in one hand and a canister labeled *NAPALM* in the other. Near the front of the parade they sang *We Shall Overcome*, swaying arm-in-arm. A guy with a beat-up guitar and long, curly hair sang Bob Dylan's *Masters of War*, and those around him joined in.   And predominant among the waving, bouncing signs above the sea of heads was the now-legendary slogan, painted in rainbow colors, surrounded by flowers and stars and hearts and tie-dye and glitter: "MAKE LOVE, NOT WAR!" Because that's what the sex, drugs and rock 'n' roll hippies in San Francisco were all about. There were few problems which couldn't be solved, or at least rendered less stressful, by liberal application of all three, preferably simultaneously. And the choice between making love and making war? Really?

Jeremy had organized the Cole Street crowd into a group of marchers, and they were shouting out the chant he and Carla and Patrick had put together a few days before. Jeremy carried a megaphone, and the group of about 15 chanted in call-and-response style.

Jeremy shouted out, "HUMANS ARE VIOLENT!"

Then he turned and pointed to his group, and they responded, "BUT THAT DON'T MAKE IT RIGHT!"

"SOMETIMES WE'RE IGNORANT!"

"BUT THT DON'T MAKE IT RIGHT!"

"AND MAYBE WE GET ARROGANT!"

"BUT THAT DON'T MAKE IT RIGHT!"

Then the whole group together: "TO MAKE THINGS RIGHT WE GOTTA STOP THE FIGHT!"

Carloads of demonstrators had driven in from L.A., Sacramento, San Diego, San Jose, Oakland, Berkeley, Marin County and hundreds of small towns all over California, determined to have their voices heard in the general uproar crying out against this unjust and catastrophic war. Among these were Carla's future husband, whom she wouldn't meet until fifteen years later, but today he was one of the marchers from L.A. He didn't share the idealism of the pacifist flower children, but grew his hair long, smoked his share of pot, went to school in Berkeley and came in protest of this particular war. He understood the concept of going to war in self-defense and saw America's participation in World War II as justified. But Vietnam was an entirely different story, with no true justification, only lies.

Hundreds of thousands of Americans were saying just that, as loudly and as often as possible. Scenes of our jets strafing the Vietnamese jungles with Napalm, killing entire villages in the name of taking out a few Viet Cong, blasted from our TV sets every night. Cargo planes full of flag-draped coffins were touching down on military bases all over the country, bringing home young soldiers who had died for absolutely nothing. The numbers of dead and horribly wounded were staggering. Minds were lost, junkies were born, lives were destroyed. The atrocities on both sides were unacceptable. All costs, financial and human, were beyond comprehension. All was *not* fair in war.

And when the group got back to Haight Street

that night, they were met with police barricades and riot cops telling them they had to go around and get to their apartments some other way. They finally got home and went upstairs and looked out the window to see what was going on. Squad cars and cops were swarming around the corner of Haight and Cole. Paddy wagons arrived carrying squads of riot cops. Carla and Patrick had pulled a curtain back and were watching as the cops formed into a military unit and began marching down Haight Street, batons in their hands. A cop on the corner, under a streetlight, turned his rifle in their direction and yelled at them to close the curtains. Shaking, they turned off the lights in their room and peeked through the curtains again. They saw cops going into every open business and shoving people out the doors, jabbing at some with their batons, yelling at everyone to get off the street and go home. Harry and Tom were watching from the upstairs window and couldn't believe their eyes. This couldn't be happening!

The next day the papers made no mention of what had happened on Haight Street or why, but word on the street was that it was some kind of marshal law, that there was a curfew which only applied to Haight Street, and that the cops were having a field day bashing hippie skulls for the crime of breathing air.

And when the street was blocked off to traffic on a weekend and the flatbed trucks were set up and the bands were blasting to a swaying, jumping crowd – when there was a sudden shockwave rolling up from Masonic toward the Cole Street corner where Carla stood listening and dancing with her friends, and half the crowd surged toward the disturbance and the other half ran for cover, she ran with the latter. A pacifist to the core, Carla swore the only advantage to being a female in this insane world was that she wouldn't have to choose between the army and prison. The worst part of the combat concept was, for her, not so much the constant dread of being killed, but the constant dread of *having to kill.* Where did the ability, even the willingness to pick up a gun and start shooting people you'd never met become a normal, healthy act?

Better dead than red? Those just couldn't be

the only two options.

11 WOODEN SHIPS

Go, take your sister then, by the hand,
Lead her away from this foreign land,
Far away, where we might laugh again,
We are leaving – you don't need us.

Wooden Ships
David Crosby, Steven Stills, Paul Kantner

In Redwood City was a group of large, dilapidated warehouses in a field of oily weeds at the edge of a slough, just a stone's throw away from the roar of the Bayshore freeway. The Tannery. It was one of those ancient buildings that housed Tom's second boat project – a 50-foot trimaran the group at the Cole Street apartment were working on together. Also parked inside, amid the sawdust and bent nails, electrical cords and hunks of dried pink epoxy was a tiny trailer where Tom and Sheela had lived while building the first boat. Every spare moment and spare dollar was devoted to the creation of this escape vehicle which Sheela had only half-jokingly dubbed the Wooden Mistress.

The atmosphere inside the old tannery was one of perpetual half-gloom, with an aroma of fiberglass resin toxic in the stagnant air. Sounds of grinding, hammering, drilling, sawing, clanging and muffled a.m. radio playing psychedelic rock filled the lofty room. Three or four boats were under construction in each building, each consuming the time, money and energy of a dreamer. Years were dedicated to planning, building, trimming, finishing and maintaining these enormous boats. Thousands of dollars were poured into plywood, hardware, power tools – the list was literally endless, with each need spawning ten more. These wooden ships were pipe dreams trying hard to come true.

Tom and the Cole Street regulars were going to sail away from the madness of the materialistic, phony twentieth century and the probable nuclear devastation we'd all been expecting since the first mushroom cloud sprouted into Earth's blue atmosphere. He would be safe with his extended family on board his vessel, sailing the high seas where no law and, hopefully, no war could reach. Maybe they'd even be fortunate enough to find the proverbial desert island where Nature made the rules – a Pitcairn of their own with no outside hookups, no morning paper to start the day off wrong, no pre-packaged food, houses or clothing, no freeways, oil refineries or billboards cluttering up the view. And all it would cost him would be several years of his life and several thousand dollars.

Brandon, too, had a smaller boat under construction alongside Tom's. David and Bob were building a sleek trimaran which was destined to cross the Pacific several times. Ron was getting his catamaran together at a snail's pace. Pete somehow managed to construct a 40-footer. And Jeb was there in his boat long before and long after anyone could remember. He lived in it, did an absolute minimum amount of work on it, and had to be removed bodily from the premises years after even the buildings had burned to the ground and the tall brick chimney had been torn down. The unfinished hull could be seen up on supports, standing in the middle of the weeds like a Christmas tree sits on the curb for weeks or months, turning brown. Jeb was so dedicated to getting loaded that he sprouted pot seeds and ate them, claiming a mild high.

Nobody believed him. But they all tried it anyway. Just in case.

Two or three mongrel dogs hung out by the tannery doors, sleeping, scratching fleas and warning the guys inside when anyone came within a mile of their turf. At sunset, these dogs would rouse themselves for the nightly hunt, dance around each other for a few minutes, then take off into the tall weeds along the water, tails waving high. They'd be back in the small hours with an aroma of dead rats wafting from their panting mouths. They slept outside, summer and winter, on the decks of boats already in the water. They'd wake up on winter mornings with frost in their fur and cat-chasing on their minds.

Brandon watched while David carefully dipped a brush into the black paint and applied it to the stern of his newly-finished boat. He made slow strokes, filling in the lines that had been lettered there, christening the trimaran *Desperado*. Brandon munched on an apple, smiling at the appropriateness of the name. He thought back to when David and Bob had decided on it.

They had all been standing around in the warehouse, having a beer in the late afternoon. The radio was tuned to its rock station, softly filling in the gaps in conversation. Brandon was cleaning his hands with a rag. David was leaning against a sawhorse, slowly sipping his beer. Bob sat on the steps of Tom's little trailer, wiping his forehead with his bandana. Tom and Sheela walked in through the partially-opened side door, with Scruffy a few paces behind. A couple of casual hellos were exchanged and Tom helped himself to a cold beer. Sheela smiled on the group and asked, "How are you desperados doin'?"

They all chuckled a little, but Brandon gave it a second thought. He glanced at David, leaning and sipping, his arms fuzzy with sawdust, his old Levi's encrusted with grime and paint – then at Bob, who wore his old cowboy bandana around his forehead and had three day's growth on his face. Brandon wondered about all of them, himself included, who worked on these boats year after year, pouring gallons of sweat onto their decks as if their very lives were at stake. David and Bob never seemed to bring any girls around. Brandon entertained thoughts that maybe they weren't interested in the opposite sex. But that didn't make much sense, either, because they both seemed to fancy themselves as lady killers, especially David. It seemed their sole interest in life was the boat and their sole pleasure, a beer and a joint at the end of the day.

Sheela went inside and started rummaging around. The radio was playing an acid rock number, shrill as glass cutting through the mellow air. Brandon walked over and flipped it off, then started in the direction of his own boat. He stopped momentarily and looked back at David.

"Hey, you know.....that wouldn't be a bad name for your boat."

David smiled blankly, but Bob asked, "What's that?"

"*Desperado,*" he replied, and walked off.

Bob and David glanced at each other, wiped the beer off their mustaches noncommittally, and went back to work on the unfinished hull that sat waiting in the dim light.

Now it was finished, months later, and they'd be putting it in the water soon. David made more careful strokes, standing on a short ladder in the mote-filled shafts of afternoon light. He was as silent as ever, concentration starting the first lines in his forehead. He made no mistakes – the lettering stood out against the white hull clear and sharp. A finishing touch, and he climbed down from the ladder and came to where Brandon was standing to survey the job. It was beautiful, in its way, and they stared in silence, each turning over the implications in his mind. One dream had just come true. A cowboy had just broken the horse he had always wanted – all that was left was to climb onto it and ride into the sunset.

A week later, David and Bob got into Bob's old truck, throwing the last of their stray belongings in the back. They had cleaned out their work area after *Desperado* was launched at high tide. Now it sat in the nearby marina, still dusty from the air of its indoor birthplace. They couldn't wait to unfurl the mainsail for the world to see. They had had it made with a large blue peace symbol sewn into its white expanse, and it gave them a rush of pride to picture it gliding under the Golden Gate Bridge on its way to the rest of their lives.

So the partners shared a joint in celebration of the event. They sat in the cab of the truck for a moment, smoke rolling out the tops of the windows, and looked at the old wooden doors of the warehouse where they had spent so many years shaping that sleek vessel, caressing its smooth surfaces and sealing it tight against the sea. Their muscles seemed to ache anew with the memory of all the nails they had pounded and sheets of plywood they had lifted into place. It was hard to believe, but it was finished. Now they could begin the planning of their maiden voyage – David has his mind set on the fair waters of Hawaii. He had turned over the trip in his head night after night, almost seeing before him the verdant islands across a stretch of silvery ocean. He had no doubts about his ability to guide this boat across the Pacific. It was only a question of time.

Bob passed the joint over to David and started up the engine. Grinning broadly, he scratched his chin and said, "All right, let's go!"

They pulled out onto the dirt road, bouncing happily toward the harbor where *Desperado* waited. On their way they passed Tom's truck, headed in the opposite direction. They waved, and Tom honked his horn in reply. Sitting next to him was Carla, coming for the first time to see what the tannery and the boat were all about – and between them on the seat, where no one could see, they held hands.

12 ALL YOU NEED

The magician, he sparkles in satin and velvet
You gaze at his splendor with eyes you've not used yet
I tell you his name is love, love, love

Sunny Googe Street
Donovan

Sausalito lies across the bay from San Francisco, affluent and picturesque and full of foggy charm. In the center of the little town sits a tiny park – a fountain surrounded by clipped grass bordered by hedges which now serve to keep out the public they once enfolded in a snug haven of momentary peace. Carla and Tom sat on the grass there one bright, windy spring noon listening to a thin black guitar player sing in his faded sarape of frayed wool. Clouds blew like kites across the window of dark blue sky as they lay and dreamed and laughed at their dreams.

Tom propped himself up on one elbow and

squinted into Carla's sleepy eyes. A roaring silence suddenly descended around them for a moment, blotting out the traffic swishing by and the guitar player and the talk and laughter of the loungers on the park grass and the blowing wind overhead. A heavy door seemed to slowly open in their minds – a door swinging on noiseless hinges, revealing behind it the naked, pure reality and telepathy of the moment.

Tom continued to stare at Carla. It was simply that he asked, knowing her answer as surely as he knew his own,

"Do you wanna do what I wanna do?"

Carla answered with a pounding heart. "Oh, yeah."

They gathered themselves upright and, brushing off their clothes and taking each others' hands, they moved off in the direction of Carla's parked truck. It sat, squat and round and swirling with paint, near the sparkling water of the docks. And as they made love inside, rocking in time with the water's lapping, the small waves rushed against the rocks of the breakwater, just as they had always done, and the foghorns moaned low and lonely out beyond the Golden Gate.

It was still a time in her life when she could cry from too much love as easily as from too little. She had been lost from that morning, shortly after meeting Tom, when they stood in the cold park amid the dripping trees and rocky acorns, huddled in their coats against the early fog, talking of small things.   Tom   turned   to   notice   two   men approaching, waving and laughing. They walked up and stood smiling at Carla with open curiosity, and then said they were going somewhere and wanted Tom to go along, just for the hell of it.   Tom shuffled his feet and brushed his fingers over his mustache and looked around on all sides and told them he couldn't go – that there were some people he had to meet and do something with, and he couldn't get out of it, sorry. The other guys hung around a few minutes, then strode off, leaving Carla with a sinking, sick feeling, as though she were being deserted by her only friend in the world.

What a jerk she had been to think Tom could spend time with her when he had a wife and family and other friends and obligations. Of course he couldn't be with her all the time, or maybe not even *some* of the time.....maybe these guys would tell his wife he was with a girl in the park. Then what? She was ashamed to look at him, to let him see the disappointment in her eyes when she clearly had no claim on him. She half-turned away from him, then said, looking at the ground,

"Well, I guess I'll see you.....?"

Tom chuckled a little and stuffed his hands deep in his pockets.

"I ain't gonna meet anybody," he said quietly.

Carla just looked at him.

"How come you told those guys you couldn't go with them?"

Tom moved a fraction closer, tilted his head thoughtfully to one side and fixed Carla with his gray-green eyes for a long moment. She had never seen this look before. It was penetrating, ripe with truth, pregnant with the kind of undivided attention she had longed for all her life but never realized until this second. Her heart squeezed in bittersweet pain with the recognition of what was coming next. She held her breath. He leaned a little closer.

"I'd rather be with you," he said.

Free Love was a phrase which implied a lot of different things to a lot of different people. To the staunch, upright, conservative American it was almost as threatening a concept as Communism or bestiality or Satan-worship. It meant nothing less than a vast, mass orgy of intertwining, naked hippie flesh and the demise of the sacred institution of marriage forever. The world would probably stop spinning and the continents would fly into space if Free Love had its degenerate, depraved way. To the college students and the beatniks it might have been some kind of Ayn Rand-esque, intellectualized way of rejecting the outdated culture of monogamy, and therefore a worthy experiment. To kids right out of high school and swarming the streets, poor but free, it was the next logical step in their rebellion against all things Establishment. It meant, literally, free sex and implied no payment, now or later. It meant ubiquitous love, love that was everywhere in the very ether, like divinity itself, and had only to be grasped to be yours. It meant your lover was just that, and not necessarily your husband or wife or old man or old lady or even your best friend. It meant you could experiment until you found the partner or group of partners that felt right, and it also meant you could change your mind about all that five minutes later. It meant couples could stray outside the marriage. *Way* outside. Men slept with men, women with women, and sometimes both at the same time. Three or four in a bed. Mix and match. Black and White and Asian and Hispanic, gay and straight and bi. It was love in the true sense of the word – people loving everything about each other and expressing it openly and often. It meant you could finally get laid, acne and all.

The birth-control pill made it possible for young women to finally go after orgasms instead of wedding rings. It was finally OK for a girl to have a libido and want a boy for is body. It was finally OK to come out of the closet and want another girl. The old concepts had to go, because they were repressive, patriarchal and double-standard. Males were supposed to have sexual needs and therefore sexual license to have premarital and even extramarital sex with impunity. Females had been told they had no such needs, and their primary sexual use was to satisfy men and have babies, and that they had to wait until they were married, lest they be forever labeled sluts. More than one couple had been forced into mismatched marriages because of a moment of lust, then forced to stay together for the sake of the accidental child. A woman could go from virgin to bride to mother to divorcee without ever knowing that sex could have been pleasurable for *her* all along. The orgasm remained a myth for some, and a guilty secret for others. But once a girl discovered the orgasm, there was no taking it away. And the young men who *really* loved them didn't want to.

Tom and Carla had broken the marriage vow. Now they had to find a way to live with whatever came next. There was guilt and fear and insecurity and confusion, but there was love. Love was supposed to conquer all. Love was a many-splendored thing. Love, according to John Lennon and Paul McCartney, was all you need. Having love allowed this generation to live in poverty, to wear rags, to go without meals, to be treated like pariahs in society, to be afraid and depressed and to come back to hope time after time because they had it and nobody could take it away. They woke up in the morning with genuine joy and enthusiasm for living when they had someone to love. And when they fell in love with someone other than their spouse, they discovered something completely unexpected: that it was possible to love more than one person at a time, and to love them each very deeply.

Carla loved Tom completely. He had given her something she had never had – an honest, open and intense caring, an undivided attention which made her feel substantial and important. He genuinely wanted to know about her thoughts and feelings. Even Patrick didn't seem to care about her in quite this way. The boys back in school had wanted what boys in school always want. Her father hadn't recognized her as an individual at all. She was merely his oldest daughter, the middle of the standard three kids, neither special like the older boy nor pampered like the younger girl. He had set the tone of how she could expect to be treated by men. He lied to her, belittled her, ignored her intellect and sensibilities, denied her an opinion, criticized her and hit her. How could she have said no to genuine love when it finally found her? She didn't even try.

13 LEARNING TO LIVE TOGETHER

And there we were all in onc place
A generation lost in space

American Pie
Don McLean

During that spring Tom arranged to rent the ten-room railroad flat on Cole Street, and he could move his family in just as soon as Wrinkleface, as the landlady was to become known, could evacuate the crashers. She sent her officious, closeted son around to chase them away, and he brought in painters to add another fresh coat to the walls and had carpet laid up the long flight of stairs and down the lightless hall.   A downstairs tenant asked Wrinkleface about the fleas left behind by the crashers. The venerable landlady, incredulous that such a thing could happen in her building, wanted to know,

"*What fleas?* There are no fleas in *my* building!"

No sooner had the words escaped her lips

than she looked down at her own scrawny legs in alarm to find them positively black with the pests. Tom said she

dropped her wrinkles as she fled down the stairs and out the front door.

Patrick and Carla were going to move in, too, renting one of the front bedrooms for $25 a month. Carla was ready to get out of the cramped truck. She was pregnant for the second time.

Her first baby, born that spring, had lived just ten days. They had moved out of their Mission District apartment a few weeks later and into a panel truck until they could find another place – anywhere but the place where the baby had died. He had simply failed to wake up one morning. She reached over to lift him from his cradle and felt his cold skin, and her heart stopped.

She had no answer for her loss, no way to even know how to think about it, no place to put the terrible sickness of grief and guilt.

In her first eighteen years, she had gone from

belief in the standard American Christian god concept – that of a gigantic man with a white beard and purple robes who lived in the clouds – to a pantheistic idea that God was another name for nature, and was everywhere – to an atheistic attitude that Man created God in his own image, which explained his human traits of jealousy, vindictiveness and violence. The death of her innocent baby put the last nail in the coffin of any lingering religious faith for her. She wanted nothing to do with a deity who created life only to destroy it, like a capricious and thoughtless child smashing toys. She saw nothing to worship.

She had dreams of a cozy room, warm and dry and off the street, where she could make a nest for herself and Patrick and the new baby. A quiet retreat.

Then she woke up.

The Cole Street apartment became a full-blown crash pad commune overnight, with all ten rooms and even the back porch off the kitchen occupied by an endless stream of people Tom had met on the street, or friends of friends of friends, fresh in from New York and Philadelphia and needing a place to stay "for a few days". Jeremy, a lanky, curly-haired 20-year-old from a wealthy family, who played guitar and talked in rhyme. Larry and Annie, a brother and sister from Brooklyn who came to see what the Haight was all about and wound up staying in San Francisco for the rest of their lives. Jimmy, who couldn't carry a tune but sang anyway, in the musty early-morning living room, smoking a hand-rolled cigarette and banging away on a cheap, timeworn guitar. Charlene, with her entourage of unsavory boyfriends slouching along the stairs at night, smoking and waiting to have a turn at her. Bernie and his cousin, Rita, who lived together until getting their own apartment on Oak Street. Joey and Julian, lovers who spread a case of the crabs around the flat. Rex and Ray, also lovers who couldn't afford pot and stopped Tom on the street to ask how to dry banana peels for smoking.

They came and went all evening, up and down the stairs, laughing and talking and playing music in the living room, cooking meals at all hours and inviting all their friends to come do it all with them.

Tom was everyone's favorite innkeeper. More than one person or couple stayed free or nearly-free. While the money from the sale of the boat lasted, he had a lot of company for dinner and went through a lot of lids of grass. Sheela was going to school at S.F. State, working toward a teaching degree. The kids were left with Tom and anyone who wanted to hang out with them. The two girls, Jenny and Libby, ran around the streets of the Haight in bare feet, playing jump rope, buying candy at the corner store, finding friends and bringing them home, just like their father.

Sean, the 4-year-old, went everywhere with Tom – running ahead on the sidewalks, hiding behind fire hydrants, chasing Scruffy's tail. He was everyone's favorite – precocious, easy to be around, curious and affectionate. Friends and family alike would take him along when they went to the store or to the park, taking pleasure in his company. This was a time and a place where trust was the rule and not the exception. Child molestation, abduction and murder were still mercifully in the future – all but unheard of and unimaginable. There was an unspoken bond between the Haight Street regulars – the street with the world's most ironic name.

The atmosphere was completely unique. They had never experienced this particular degree of civility and familiarity before, and much to their heartbreak, would never experience it again. Complete strangers would greet each other on the sidewalks and be deep in conversation within seconds, instinctively trusting, telepathically sharing and openly welcoming. Boys and girls kissed and hugged without knowing each others names. Groups shared a joint, a bottle a sandwich without the fear of germs we now seem to obsess over. Kids rollerskated and rode their bikes up and down the streets all day without a kneepad or a helmet among them. Hitchhiking was not seen as a dangerous activity – it was a mode of transportation. And contrary to the wildly-successful propaganda campaign against marijuana which lives on today – the potheads drifting up and down the neighborhood were hardcore peaceniks who wanted nothing less than to rid the world of all violence, forever.

Carla's mother cornered her during a visit and worriedly asked her if she wasn't afraid she'd "get addicted" to pot. She had obviously believed the stories and pictured Carla winding up in the gutter, destitute and craving her next fix. Carla told her,

"It's not like that, it's not addictive, it's something you do sometimes, don't do other times, no problem. We don't *have to have it.* If it's there, fine, if not, that's OK too. And it doesn't take more and more to get you high – I smoke the same amount every time and get the same effect. And I do *not* want to do harder drugs! I swear! All that other stuff is available to me, but I don't want it. Pot is enough."

She knew her mother didn't believe her. She could only hope that as the years passed and she remained normal, healthy and able to make it through the day without ingesting any drugs whatsoever that her mom would finally get it.

In the end, it wasn't societal pressure or the

judgment of parents that made her stop smoking – it was the advent of sinsemilla – a speedy, paranoia-producing grass that bore little resemblance to the mellow, happy, sensual high they used to know and love. Propaganda films like *Reefer Madness* depicted madness all right – the madness of the filmmakers whose imaginations must have been supercharged by the same drugs they sought, perhaps more than a bit cynically, to eradicate. The scenes depicted were so psychedelic in themselves – the manner in which the character holds the reefer in cupped, trembling hands, taking quick, shallow puffs (without inhaling), rolling his eyes like a Hollywoodized, hyperbolized madman, then slashing someone to death with a knife just for fun – these scenes were so patently fantasized the filmmakers had to have been high on *something* when they were created. But square, conformist America saw them as documentaries, admonishing their kids to stay away from the killer weed *or else,* while lighting another Lucky Strike and throwing back another Miller High Life. Marijuana was christened the "gateway drug", meaning its use inevitably led to harder drugs, as evidenced by the "fact" that all hard drug users had at one time smoked pot.

Carla, talking to Rose one hazy afternoon in the kitchen, put it this way:

"First of all there is no gateway drug. The gateway exists in your brain. You're either going to get heavy into drugs or you're not, and a mountain of free cocaine means nothing if you don't *like* cocaine." (Carla didn't like cocaine, which made her very popular at parties during the 80's). "But if you're looking for the beginnings of drug addiction, look at caffeine, nicotine and alcohol.....all legal, all addictive. Parents think *nothing* of letting their kids drink Coca-Cola all day, and then they almost *expect* them to start smoking when they're in high school, since that's what *they* did. And of course everyone smokes and drinks by the time they're out of school. How many junkies and coke freaks went straight from milk and cookies to mainlining smack – without coffee, cigarettes and beer somewhere in between? Junkies have smoked pot because *junkies do drugs* – not the other way around."

The streetcorner preacher shouted out to the crowd passing by, his face red and his neck veins popping.

"Watch out!" Watch out for the weed with roots in Hell – maree – wanna! Your kids are committing only God knows what kinda sins! Your sweet little baby girls are taking that maree-wanna and letting men have their way with `em and pretty soon they're walking the streets! They're *harlots* and *hoors* and sinful in the eyes of the Lord! All because they got that maree-wanna monkey on their back! They need more and more and *more* to get their kicks! It's the Devils' weed, I tell you – *Satan* is making them smoke it and it's *dragging your kids down into Hell!*"

"We don't believe in Satan!" Carla said loudly.

The preacher ignored her. He waved his bible in one hand and pointed a long, bony finger with the other and glared at the hippies watching with folded arms and lazy smiles. Tom and Carla walked a few paces closer, then a few paces closer, and Tom reached over and embraced the preacher with a big hug while Carla joined the spectators in appreciative laughter. The preacher froze, his face turned even deeper red and he pushed Tom away furiously, scowling and cursing.

"Hey," Tom said, "doesn't that bible you're holding tell everybody to love their neighbor? C'mon, brother, show us how much you love your fellow man....."

But the preacher turned and ran, shaking as he went as if to rid himself of the very demons of Hell, brushing his clothes of the contamination of having had another man touch him, his face redder than ever. Tom and Carla watched him go, smiling.

"So much for brotherly love," said Carla. "If he had a gun instead of a bible, you'd be dead right now."

"The bible might as well be a gun," said Tom. "It's used as a weapon, after all. It's used like a cage to put people in, like chains to tie 'em to a wall and like a rack to torture 'em on. Feel guilty! Feel like shit! God wants you to suffer!"

"And give us money, while you're at it," said Carla.

"Yeah," Tom laughed. "Jesus needs money. Why can't he just, ya know, print his own? Isn't he supposed to be able to do anything? Hey! I'm outta money! I'll just make some more.....POOF!"

They sat down on a bus-stop bench.

"The Mormons are supposed to give ten percent of their income to the church," said Carla. "They make you do it with guilt, because everybody knows everybody else's business in that church. It's all about status and who's a better Mormon than whom. How many times you go to Sunday School and how you're dressed once you get there is way more important than what you really believe or what kind of human being you are. And of course, they're the "chosen people". Interestingly enough, so are the Jews and the Muslims and every other goddamn religious sect on Earth. All but one of them has got to be wrong."

Just then, a group of yellow-robed, shaven-headed Hare Krishnas came dancing down the sidewalk, chanting and beating on tambourines and asking for donations.

"Yeah," said Tom, "religion really solves everything. If we just kill a Commie for Christ, everything will be fixed!" You'd think, after all the fuckin' wars we've fought since time began, all the things we were fighting over would be *resolved* by now.....otherwise, what was it all about?"

"I hear ya," said Carla. "They're killing each other by the thousands in Vietnam, but when it's over and done and all those corpses have turned into so much fertilizer, does that mean we've actually *learned* something and don't have to do it again? What's that line about when you don't learn anything from history you're doomed to repeat it? What do you wanna bet this isn't the last war we'll have to protest against in our lifetimes?"

"Holy shit," said Tom. "I just hope Sean's not the right age to get drafted if *that* ever happens!"

"I'll help you hide him," said Carla.

They headed back to Cole Street, and along the way they met a couple of kids needing a place to crash for the night, and they took them home.

Your choice is simple: join us and live in peace, or pursue your present course and face obliteration. We shall be waiting for your answer. The decision rests with you.

Klaatu
The Day the Earth Stood Still

"Whatcha readin', Jeremy? Carla said.

"Huh?" he said with his head in the fridge.

"What's the book?" She pointed to it with her sandwich. The title read, *The Interrupted Journey.*

"Oh, man. You *gotta* read this thing. It's about this couple in New Hampshire who got, like *kidnapped* by *aliens.....*"

"You mean little green men from Mars?" Tom laughed.

"I'm not talking about some work of *fiction* here, you guys," Jeremy said, stuffing his sandwich full of alfalfa sprouts. "This is for real. They didn't even know what happened to them until they got hypnotized later on. Then they remembered that these humanoids with really big eyes grabbed `em off some country road....."

"Now why," Carla put in, "is it always somebody *else* who gets to see these things? How come they never land in Golden Gate Park so *we* could see them?"

"Carla, Carla, Carla!" said Jeremy, "They don't land in the middle of Golden Gate Park or on the White House lawn or in any other public place for one simple reason." He paused for effect, leaning forward to look into her eyes. "If they knew enough about Earth to *get* here, right?, then they've *gotta* know what a bunch of bloodthirsty bastards we are and that they'd be shot down on the spot. They certainly didn't come all this way – from wherever – to commit suicide."

He leaned back in his chair. "All the science

fiction movies we saw when we were kids were right on, man. The flying saucer lands, and the first thing everybody does is call the goddamn U.S. Army to bring out the heavy artillery and start firing. Nobody asks questions, except for the absent-minded professor and his cute daughter in the pointy bra, and her boyfriend, who winds up saving the day, single-handed. The American military, true to form, never finds out what they might want – they just waste `em and pat each other on the back for "saving the world".

"Yeah," said Tom. "Maybe they're here to give us the cure for cancer or something, and we blow their heads off before they even turn off the engine....."

"Correctomundo," said Jeremy. "We're a bunch of arrogant assholes – we can't live with the idea that *perhaps* there are other beings out there with other ideas....."

"And how come these aliens always look like humans?" Carla said. "I mean, how imaginative is *that?* Are we really so egocentric we think all intelligent life has to look like *us?*"

"Yes," said Tom, "we *are.*"

"I like some of the stuff in *Childhood's End,*" said Carla, "when he talks about this kid who has dreams about planets where the only life forms are these moving crystals....."

"Yeah," said Tom, "and what about the aliens – when people finally saw them? They turned out to look like Satan?"

Jeremy sighed. "I think these guys look like humans because they *are* humans."

The other two raised their eyebrows.

"I think," Jeremy went on, "these so-called aliens are really just humans. They're not from another planet. They're people coming back from the *future.*"

"Then what's with the big eyes?" said Carla.

"Evolution,"   said   Jeremy.   "*Intentional*

evolution. Humans don't evolve anymore because we don't need to. We don't have to adapt to nature because we make nature adapt to us. We kill off all the natural predators we can with weapons. We don't have to grow fur anymore because we wear clothes....."

"Yeah," said Carla, "including the fur of *other* animals."

"And," Jeremy went on, "we build air-conditioned and heated buildings so we don't have to deal with all that – we don't have to worry about dying of exposure to the elements anymore. Women with access to hospitals don't die in childbirth anymore, and the babies live, too, thanks to medical intervention. We're living longer and longer.....but I think that in the future, people are gonna figure out a way to play around with our own genes and stuff so we'll be able to survive the slow death of the *rest* of nature.....and the big eyes are to protect us from the sunlight, which will be too intense because we've destroyed the atmosphere.

"Oh, man," said Tom. "We're gonna have to make different lungs so we can breathe all the poison that's in the air. And how about the garbage in the water we drink and the pesticides all over our food?"

"Don't forget *quick* death from nuclear war," said Carla. "Somehow, I don't think the duck-and-cover thing is *quite* enough to protect you from a *hydrogen bomb*. Remember when we were in school, and they used to have the air raid drills – you'd hear a yellow alert siren and then a red-alert siren.....where were these sirens *located?*.....Anyway, then we'd jump under our desks and put our hands over our heads, like that would prevent 40 megatons of nuclear firestorm from turning us into a teaspoonful of ash. I used to wake up in the middle of the night, and I heard those sirens! I'd see lights on the ceiling of my room and hear noises, like a tank coming down the street, and I'd be scared shitless, thinking it was the Russians! I later found out it was the street-sweeper truck, which came in the middle of the night `cause there were fewer cars parked on the street then. Jesus!"

They sat for a while chewing their sandwiches. Jeremy picked up his book, Tom leaned over and lit a cigarette on the gas burner of the stove. Carla gazed out the window into the afternoon haze.

"You know," she said, "the idea of getting kidnapped by aliens reminds me of something out of *The Wind in the Willows* – a chapter where the rat and the mole are looking for a lost baby otter....."

"What?" laughed Tom. "Is this a fairy-tale book or somethin'?"

"Well," she said, "supposedly. But it's right up *my* boulevard. It's like *Alice in Wonderland* – written by a British guy for British children a long time ago, so naturally it's way over the heads of modern American kids. Anyway, the rat and the mole come across this satyr, this pan, in a forest clearing, and are totally awestruck by the sight. He's, like, a god to the animals. Then the vision disappears and they can't remember having seen him. But for a while, they're trying to remember – like when you're trying to remember a nice dream you were right in the middle of. But they can't. It's the pan's gift to them – to make them forget what they've seen so they can, you know, live in the *real* world again without going nuts over the nirvana they felt but can't re-experience."

Jeremy looked at Carla. "What was the pan called, in the book?"

"The Piper at the Gates of Dawn."

"Wow. There's an album by Pink Floyd by that name. Just came out – I saw it in the record store the other day."

"*Really?*" said Carla. "Jesus, there must be something in the air!"

Tom laughed. "Nothing you two say can surprise me anymore." He reached over and squeezed Carla's hand.

"Hey," Jeremy went on, "you may be onto something with that whole connection. The aliens, in this book anyway, have the ability to block people's memories – but it's not just because they don't want to be found out – they're actually being *humane* by keeping people from remembering this traumatic event. They know how emotional we are, and how this kind of thing could drive us completely nuts."

"You know," said Carla, "I can't remember my whole first-grade year. I can remember *before* and *after,* but not a damn thing from when I was six. Except maybe this dream I had....."

"You can remember a dream from when you were *six?"* said Tom. "I can barely remember what I dreamed last night!"

"I guess the reason I remember it is because it scared me so bad I thought I was going to die, and I never was really sure it was a dream....."

"Nightmares'll do that," said Jeremy.

"Actually, it was my mother who said it was a dream, not me," said Carla.

"Well, what do *you* think it was?" said Tom.

"That's just it," said Carla. "I don't remember anything about the dream itself – just *after* it. I ran down the hall to my parents' bedroom and sort of whimpered that there was a man with a flashlight who was trying to kill me. Funny thing is, I've had flashbacks of this tactile sensation from this thing – a kind of sickening feeling that involves a cylindrical metal object. And, you know, at the time of the dream, I didn't really feel that the man was a man or the flashlight was a flashlight, but those were the only words I could come up with at that age. And I felt the strange reluctance to even tell my mom about it, as if it was supposed to be a secret. And right after this happened, I was *afraid of the sky.*"

She got up to put her dishes in the sink.

"Holy shit," said Jeremy. "You haven't read this book, have you? The aliens did medical experiments on these people and used metal probes.....and later they were afraid of stuff and they didn't know why....."

"Whew," said Tom, and laughed.

Jeremy got up and stretched his long frame.

"Anyway," he said, "The reason the aliens don't land in a big crowd of people in a major city is that we have the unfortunate combination of stupidity and violent behavior and they know it.....either they come from an intellectually-superior *place* or an intellectually-superior *time*. The key word is "superior".

He kissed the top of Carla's head and strolled out the door.

Sheela was coming down the hall with the two girls. They had been to the grocery store and had cookies sticking out the top of the brown-paper bags.

"Quick!" said Tom, reaching over to intercept a bag on its way to the pantry shelf. "Let's get these Oreos before the party starts."

"Party?" said Sheela.

"You never know," said Tom.

15 THESE FRIENDS OF MINE

I wish, I wish, I wish in vain
That we could sit simply in that room again
Ten thousand dollars at the drop of a hat
I'd give it all gladly if our lives could be like that

Bob Dylan's Dream
Bob Dylan

No birthday or housewarming or graduation was necessary anymore to have a party, as the definition had changed – in fact, "party" was now both a noun and a verb, and the only excuse anyone needed was that the sun had gone down. Three or more people in the living room after 9 pm was a good start, and if someone was playing a guitar, and someone else was rolling a joint, then it was official.

Patrick and Larry played their guitars, Sheela played an autoharp, Carl sang with them and played the harmonica, and there was always someone to blow into the gallon wine bottle for jug-band songs. There were no televisions in the house. They had all grown up with the little black-and-white box in the living room, around which the family would gather every single night after dinner. The kids went to bed after a certain program was over. (That was the beginning of an entire nation changing its schedule around to fit television programming). The blue glow continued to flicker in the room and the canned audience continued laughing for the unhearing, sleeping mom and dad in their recliners. Television quickly filled the time that used to be occupied by such quaint pastimes as conversation, reading, game-playing, listening to the radio, sewing and working on hobbies. After a few short years of watching TV every night from dinner to bedtime, people forgot what they had done with those hours before. Most never went back to life without TV – they died fifty years later, asleep forever in front of the flickering screen.

Carla, Patrick, Tom, Sheela and the rest had other things to do with their time – would have described them as *better* things – and felt no loss from the lack of TV. They all read books for pleasure. They were either listening to music or making it. Almost every night was a songfest, and everyone in the room had some degree of talent for singing and playing. Larry and Patrick were professional-grade guitarists, both self-taught, and Jeremy was classically trained and could always take the instrumental solo between verses, bending notes and bending heads. Carla had taught herself the basic guitar chords when she was sixteen, learning to play along with the Beatles, Peter, Paul and Mary, and even some of the easier Dylan songs. She and Sallie and Robert had discovered the joys of the Marine Band harmonica in the key of E, and they had holders for playing guitar and harmonica simultaneously. Sheela had a powerful voice as she leaned over her autoharp and moaned the old folk tunes with real pathos. Larry and Patrick took requests from the room, always getting an enthusiastic reaction with jug-band numbers by Jim Kweskin and John Sebastian. None of them ever needed a reason for all the music – it was innate, part of their DNA, and they couldn't have imagined their lives without its constant presence.

Strangers from the street wandered up the stairs and down the hall to where the music was playing, and picked a spot on one of the couches, intercepted the joint or the wine jug, or joined in the singing or the rhythm section, tapping a spoon against a glass or just clapping in time. One guy came in wearing a big, ragged fur coat and carrying a shopping bag full of psychedelic comics to pass out to the room. A girl dressed in black, her bare feet blue from the night cold, appeared from the doorway – she went over to where Tom sat smoking and took his hands, saying, "Dance with me – there's a full moon and witches always dance under a full moon!"

As they twirled around the room, she began shedding her clothes, tossing them in the air, until Sheela gently reminded her of the kids in the room.

Late one night, a small, intense-looking man and two girls with long brown hair showed up in the room and sat down cross-legged on the floor, smiling and nodding. Carla sensed something strange about the three, and watched them from under her hair as she strummed the guitar. He had a goatee and shoulder-length dark hair and the most intense eyes she had ever seen – they were piercing – and when he caught her looking at him, his smile vanished and he jumped up, striding across the room to stand over her threateningly. He glared down at her with his arms folded like a genie from a bottle. Carla couldn't take it and scrambled off the couch, rushing out of the room and down the hallway to her bedroom, leaving the door open a crack so she could see when these three left. It wasn't long before she saw them head down the stairs in a cloud of incense from the sticks the girls were carrying. When she heard the front door slam, she went back into the living room. There was a break between songs. She held up her hands in question.

"What was *that?*"

Patrick and Tom shook their heads.

"Creepy vibes!" said Tom.

"That guy was *dangerous.*" said Patrick.

"Who the hell *were* they?" said Carla. "Did you see the way that guy was looking at me? Made my skin crawl!"

"I dunno," said Patrick.

Little Sean, playing with a toy truck on the floor, said, without looking up, "He said his name was Charlie."

Carla stared down at the top of Sean's head, then looked back at Tom.

"Maybe we should *lock* the fucking *door*."

Through it all – before the music, after the music, even during the music – they *talked to each other*. At length, and with keen interest, attention and empathy. They talked about relationships and institutions and politics and religion and about the bloody, mindless war which was killing their brothers and their friends. They opened their hearts to each other, leaned on each other, helped each other, and they loved each other the best they could. They were trying to overthrow the old, conformity-based systems which cut everyone from the same cloth, and monogamy was one of those. They had all been taught, repeatedly and without equivocation, that all people were meant to find a mate of the opposite sex, marry, have children and remain together for the rest of their lives, period. (Their parents preached it, but didn't always practice it. Divorce had been considered scandalous not that long ago, and now it was becoming almost commonplace. Some kids had even *wished* their parents would divorce, if it meant an end to the constant dysfunction and fighting). There was no room in the script for more than two people in a marriage – indeed, even casual boyfriend/girlfriend relationships were based on the idea of possessive monogamy. There was no room for a woman living alone or for anyone to remain single and childless by choice. Marriage and children were supposed to fulfill all needs, especially for women, since it should always be understood that men have "greater" needs than women and therefore aren't so easily satisfied. Men were expected to stay in the marriage, but women were expected to *want to* stay in the marriage.

Other lifestyle scenarios, too deviant to imagine, were beginning to emerge from the freedom of the sixties, but were still in the future of mainstream consciousness. Cross-dressing was shocking enough, but the very idea of gender-reassignment surgery would have killed the average conservative.   The   dirty   secret   that   same-sex couples even existed was horrible enough – but that they would some day be given the same legal rights as married couples, or that they might actually be allowed   to   adopt   children   was   completely unthinkable.   Such twisted, perverted behavior was seen as a sin against the god which conservative, mainstream America claimed to believe in, and a threat   to   the   sacred   institution   of   traditional matrimony.   It   was   widely   believed   that   if   gay couples were allowed to exist it would mean the demise of normal, one-man-one-woman marriage forever – which would lead to the ultimate demise of civilization.   Precisely how this chain of events would unfold has never been rationally explained (since it can't be) but presumably, if a hypothetical Bruce and Stan were allowed to live together as lovers and have sexual intercourse in the privacy of their bedrooms under cover of darkness, the very *concept* in the minds of the heretofore-happily-married heterosexual couple next door would be enough to break them apart like a crisp breadstick. Just   *imagining*   two   men   having   sex   would traumatize the rest of the world so intensely and irreparably that all couples, everywhere, would divorce each other on the spot, and that couples contemplating marriage would instantly change their minds, might even decide to *become gay themselves!* They wouldn't be able to help it, now that Bruce and Stan were doing it. Bruce and Stan's criminal behavior would spread, like a pandemic, into the otherwise-decent minds of all Americans and fester there, causing people to drop all upstanding, righteous ideals they once held and start copulating with members of the same gender. And from there it's a short slide down the proverbial slippery slope toward incest, bestiality and complete moral collapse. Better to stay in a loveless, soul-crushing, repressive, abusive and degrading marriage than turn queer. Better to kill yourself and spare your family irreparable shame and disgrace than to make your queerness public. Society was positive that God would punish these sinners later, but sometimes wasn't willing to wait that long, and decided to go ahead and punish them now.

Back in reality, they were in their 20's. It was

the Summer of Love. Drugs were everywhere, and drugs break down inhibitions. Girls were braless and on birth control pills. Guys were gorgeous with their long hair and tight pants. Everyone was high on hormones. It was like a giant candy store, and the idea of monogamy became ridiculous to a 20-year-old. One person for the rest of your life?

For them, this was the life they had been born to live, at least while they were young, and they lived it with everything they had, making it up as they went along, taking the pain along with the pleasure.

Sex, drugs and rock 'n' roll? Hell, yes! There would be plenty of time for abstinence, rehab and elevator music later on.

16 BACK TO THE GARDEN

We are stardust, we are golden
We are caught in the devil's bargain
And we've got to get ourselves back to the garden...

Woodstock
Joni Mitchell

Ashton Bright put it this way: "No true hippie woman ever carries a purse."

He was holding forth for the crowd, standing on his wire milk basket, speaking into a megaphone.

"And," he went on, "this is an absolute. This is true one hundred percent of the time. If a woman carries a purse, she cannot be counted among bona fide, genuine, card-carrying hippies. Nor, I might add, does a true hippie woman ever shave her legs or her armpits, wear makeup (with the exception, of course, of dayglo paint on special occasions), wear stockings or heels or slips or – God forbid – *girdles!*"

This got a big hand from the crowd. Carla turned to Patrick.

"Yeah I used to wear one of those things. When I was, like, fourteen and didn't *need* to."

"Now, as for bras....." Ash went on, pausing with a raised eyebrow for effect.

The girls and women sitting around him on the grassy slope booed and jeered on cue. A voice from the rear squealed out,

"FUCK BRAS!"

"Ah, but that's the problem," said Ash, raising his arms in supplication. "Nobody wants to when you're wearing one."

Appreciative applause from the men.

"Really now. Can any self-respecting hippie girl really expect any self-respecting hippie guy to take her seriously when she's wearing her Maidenform?"

Carla was near the front, so she didn't have to yell too loudly, "They don't take us seriously, anyway!"

"Right on!" came the squealer from the back.

Everyone was laughing. Ash fixed a big grin on Carla, folded his arms, and waited until the noise died down. Then he raised his megaphone to his mouth.

"SO – you wear a bra, huh?"

Carla collapsed, laughing, against Patrick. Ash ran his fingers through his beard thoughtfully. "OK, so we've established who's a real hippie and who's not. What else does a real hippie not do?"

"Get a haircut!" came the voice of a 16-year-old with his blonde hair in his eyes.

"Watch TV!" someone yelled.

"Eat meat!"

Aha!" said Ashton. "Now you've hit upon what might be the essence of hipness. I mean, it's common knowledge that eating meat makes you violent, right? Just look at the Hell's Angels!"

He shot a few furtive glances around, in case any were within earshot. "Those guys eat a diet of raw meat, and look at *them.* They've got a bad attitude! Now, if they were to change over to bean sprouts and carrots, who knows?"

From the edge of the crowd a guy wearing colors called out good-naturedly, "Hey, we *cook* our meat before we eat it!"

Laughter all around. "Maybe, said Ash, but do you *kill it* before you cook it?"

The guy just nodded his head, laughing. Ashton turned back to the audience. "I have to confess," he said, "I actually had a hamburger the other day....."

Loud booing from the crowd. Someone threw a half-eaten carrot. Ash held up his hand for silence.

"Not only did I eat a hamburger.....I ate a hamburger at McDonald's!"

With that declaration, he made a pretense of running for cover and protecting his head with his arms. Several people even stood up to boo, and there were cries of "Turncoat!" and "Get the rope!"

When things had calmed down, the kid with the hair in his eyes said, laughing, "That's fucked up, man! That shit is *plastic!*"

Ashton hung his head in mock shame. "I know it," he said quietly. "It is *really* fucked up. I need help with this problem. Maybe I should go to a shrink or something." He looked up. "Is there a shrink in the house?"

Out on Stanyan Street, a van was driving by with a sticker on its bumper: "Love Your Animal Friends.....Don't Eat Them."

And it was about this moment when Larry was choking on a plum that his guru had told him to swallow whole to cleanse his system of all impurities. Larry was embarking on a quest. He thought perhaps the road to Nirvana, the ultimate pleasure, could be shortcut by depriving himself of any pleasure through food. He was already celibate, meditating four hours a day, saying his mantra in the bathtub. Now he attacked his desire and materialism from within. He found a guru who had been speaking in the park one day, visited the ashram, paid a few bucks toward the cause and took up the purification diet.

So now he was trying to swallow this strange, salty plum that had been in a jar on some musty shelf in China for several centuries. It wasn't all that big, true, but he regarded it with fear as he worked up the courage to swallow it. Sarah and Carol were there in the kitchen, stirring up something for lunch, and Sarah couldn't contain her curiosity.

"What the hell is *that?*" she said, eyeing the puckered, black ball.

"It's a special plum, for purifying the body, ya

know?" said Larry.

"Looks disgusting. Couldn't you just take some X-Lax or something?"

Larry clucked his tongue impatiently. "Nah! You gotta swallow it whole, and it....."

"You gotta *what?*"

"SHH!" said Larry, closed his eyes, and placed it on his tongue. The vile taste told him this just had to be poison. But, visualizing the benevolent face of his guru, he summoned one last rush of courage and swallowed. It got a few inches down, and stopped. Instantly, Larry broke out in a cold sweat. The thought of dying in the process of trying to improve his life was too much. Sarah and Carol stared as Larry went through the motions of trying to inhale. He turned red. Sarah's eyes got very wide.

"Holy shit!" she said, "he's choking!"
"Slap him on the back!" said Carol, jumping from her chair and running over.

Sarah whacked him on the shoulder blades, nearly knocking him over, but not dislodging the plum. Then, out of desperation, she put her arms around his middle and squeezed. At last he coughed, meaning the thing had either come up or gone down. His knees buckled and he fell to the kitchen floor, coughing. Carol got some water from the sink and brought it to him. He waved her away, still unable to speak. He never wanted to put anything in his mouth again, not even water. He sat there, feeling that damn plum glide slowly down his gullet and into his stomach, were it sat like a stone.

Twenty-four hours later he thought he might die again, as he went to the bathroom and the plum came out. Still whole.

Larry walked around the apartment with a tiny brown bag full of organic brown rice, eating it grain by raw grain. And he ate very little else. Everything was so impure, you see. All the stuff from the supermarket was covered with pesticide, grown in soil that had been chemically fertilized, and probably preserved with some cancer-causing agent that the government was keeping secret. The guru said you should grow your own food – that way you would know what was in it. You couldn't even trust the health-food stores. Larry had dreams of turning over the soil to the sun and harvesting the crop he'd grown with his own hands. First he'd have to find the right commune out in the country. One that had real positive vibes. One where everyone could all live together and be self-sufficient and not have to ever go to the store and buy plastic food. Maybe he'd meet a nice girl and they'd have a couple of kids and just live the way nature intended.

He'd heard of communes in the country – up in Humboldt County and around Napa Valley, places like Sunshine Farm. He talked to Patrick and Carla about it, and one weekend they decided to go check it out. It was only a couple of hours away, up near Santa Rosa. They had to hitchhike, as usual, and lucked into a ride with someone who was going almost right there. They climbed out of the pickup truck in one of those small California towns – they all have a general store, where the locals congregate, and a gas station, where the tourists get ripped off.

An old man in overalls was sitting on the store steps. A big red dog slept at his feet. They went inside to ask directions. There was a young boy behind the wood counter, about thirteen. He was tall and fat, and his white t-shirt was torn. He looked at them with naked suspicion. They looked like damn hippies. Patrick and Larry both had straight, longish hair, big sideburns and full mustaches. Patrick wore a shirt with a tie-dyed peace symbol on the front. Larry had his guitar slung across his back. Carla wore Levi's and a purple peasant blouse, and her blonde hair hung to her waist.

"Hi," said Patrick. "Do you know how to get to Sunshine Farm?"

"Huh?" said the boy.

"I can tell you how to get there," came a voice from behind them. It was the old man from the front steps. He was leaning against the door frame, and he looked up eagerly at each of them, smiling in a pained way. He gestured toward the road outside.

"Ya go north here.....then you'll see a row of mailboxes. Well, one big one with all the flowers painted on it is the one for Sunshine. Just turn right and go up the road about 2 miles. You'll know it when you get there. Place smells like mareewanna!"

His cigarette laugh turned into a hacking cough as he went back outside. The boy sniggered at this last remark. Carla looked at him, and he stopped.

"Well, thanks," said Patrick.

The three of them walked out into the sunshine and down the steps. As they crossed the road, they heard someone behind them clear his throat dramatically and spit. They didn't look back.

There was no one to greet them at the wobbly wooden gates of Sunshine. They saw two men out in a fenced-in area, pulling at something on the ground. There was a run-down, shingled house hidden behind several parked cars and a big school bus that had been painted dayglo orange. Everything was covered with dust. It was quiet except for the buzzing of insects. Carla looked around and noticed a big tipi pitched among the yellow weeds on a slope behind the house. The silence was broken by a child crying. They ventured through the open door into the dark house and saw a toddler, about 18 months old, sobbing in the middle of the room. He had on a little t-shirt and nothing else. Carla immediately started looking around for his mother. Then they heard women talking and a darkly-tanned woman with long, tangled black hair emerged with a large mixing bowl in her hands.

"Oh, hi," she said vaguely. Then she wandered back in the direction from which she had come. It must have been the kitchen. Carla raised her hands.

"What the fuck?" she whispered.

Larry shrugged. Patrick giggled. The baby was still whimpering, looking at them tragically and sucking his thumb. Suddenly the woman with the bowl appeared again.

"C'mere, Jedediah," she said roughly.

The little boy waddled over and she took his hand. She led him over to a small dusty rag rug and told him to sit down. Then she handed him a small bowl filled with nuts and a nutcracker, and left the room again. The child looked at the bowl, then at Carla, then back again. Patrick and Larry wandered around the room, looking at the shabby, threadbare furniture, the fireplace, black with wood ash, the buds of home-grown pot left out in the open. Patrick picked up a book from a table and Larry sat down on the torn upholstery of the secondhand couch, took out his guitar and started strumming softly.

Carla went over to the little boy, sat down on the floor next to him and began to crack nuts and hand them to him. The mother came rushing into the room. She stood over Carla with her hands on her hips and demanded,

"Leave my kid alone!"

Carla looked up, shocked. "I was helping him

eat these nuts....."

"He doesn't need any help!   He can do it himself.   How else will he learn, if somebody's always doing it *for* him? Gotta cut the apron strings *sometime!*"

"But," Carla said, "he's just a baby. He doesn't look strong enough....."

"Look," said the woman, "I don't even know who the fuck you are. But he's *my* kid, not yours, so just leave him alone!"

Larry had stopped playing, and got up and walked out the door, with Patrick following behind. Carla said nothing, stood up and gave the woman what she hoped was a sufficiently-disapproving look. The kid had resumed crying as she went outside.

They looked around. There was a small, weedy vegetable garden by the side of the dirt driveway, its sparse crop wilting in the baking sun. Two guys in jeans were leaning against an old outbuilding behind the garden, smoking cigarettes and drinking beer. They waved but didn't move. The heat sat on the afternoon like a heavy blanket. Flies and mosquitoes buzzed around Carla's arms, making her swat furiously. Larry wiped his head with a bandana and sighed.

"I don't know about this living-off-the-land thing," he said with a little chuckle.

"Yeah," said Carla. "It doesn't look like anybody's having much fun. That veggie garden looks pretty pathetic. I wonder how many people are here, anyway? It doesn't look like enough to live on....."

Patrick appeared from behind them, smoking a joint. Suddenly, the stillness was broken by sounds of someone yelling down by a chicken-wire fence. They headed that way, wondering what was going on. As they got closer, they could see it was a guy wearing nothing but a pair of dirty corduroy shorts, his light-brown hair grown into dreadlocks from long neglect. His skin was rough and brown and streaked with sweat and dust. He held a little brown bag in one hand, and grains of brown rice spilled from it onto the dirt and weeds. Carla looked pointedly at Larry, who shrugged.

A few other people had appeared, and stood staring.

"What's wrong with him?" someone asked.

A man with glasses and long braids stood over the guy moaning and babbling on the ground and said, "It's nothing. He's just going through ego death."

"Oh," said the first one. "Cool."

Carla, Patrick and Larry exchanged looks. Larry raised is eyebrows as if to say, *what??* Patrick just stared, taking another toke on his joint. Carla grabbed them by the arms and pulled them a few steps back.

"Hey, you guys, let's get outta here," said Carla.

"Yeah," said Patrick, "this place is givin' me

bad vibes."

They turned and trudged back up the slope of the rutted dirt driveway, headed for the road.

"Ego death?" said Carla. "What in the hell is that supposed to even mean?" I'm no doctor, but it looked more like a combination of sunstroke and vitamin deficiency to me. Do people really think they can live on just brown rice – no offense, Larry – and nothing else?"

"I'm over the brown rice thing," said Larry. "It was bullshit. You gotta have protein. As soon as we get home, let's go to Zim's for a burger!"

"Now you're talkin," said Patrick. "Wouldn't want your ego to die!"

They all laughed, passing the joint around as they walked toward the highway and a ride back to the City.

17 FEED YOUR HEAD

One pill makes you larger
And one pill makes you small
And the ones that Mother gives you
Don't do anything at all

White Rabbit
Grace Slick

Patrick wandered into the corner head shop, the Psyche-Deli, to pick up some Zig Zags. This was the place to buy supplies – the paraphernalia necessitated by getting loaded on a regular basis. Here you could read "adult" comic books or even catch up on your meditation in an incense-filled, mattress-strewn room behind beaded curtains. Lining the walls were large posters of the rock legends of the day. Jimi Hendrix with headband and bare chest, playing his guitar with his tongue. Janis Joplin screaming her guts out, feather boa drenched in Southern Comfort-scented sweat. Bob Dylan scowling out from under his carefully-messed-up hair. Fillmore and Avalon Ballroom bills of fare, announcing Cream, Steve Miller, the Iron Butterfly,

Quicksilver Messenger Service, Buffalo Springfield, the Youngbloods, the Greatful Dead, Big Brother and the Holding Company, Blue Cheer, the Jefferson Airplane. Black-light posters and ultraviolet light tubes to go with them. Zodiac posters, Kama Sutra charts, mandalas, poetry booklets, pot-cultivation guides and grow lights. Leisure time that previously had been spent on the backyard patio with a can of beer was now being spent smoking grass and taking pills and watching the inner movie roll out.

Many an hour was spent pouring over the wit and wisdom between the covers of Zap Comix, Freak Brothers and Mr. Natural. Characters such as Angelfood McSpade, Flakey Foont, Fritz the Cat and Whiteman muddled through situations that usually revolved around getting loaded, getting laid and wringing Truth from the existential crises of modern urban life. Motorcycle gang members blew each other off silver choppers with flaming gas tanks. Speedfreaks cringed in the dark corners of tenement slums. Upstanding citizens got their minds blown by the antics of Robert Crumb's irrepressible characters. The sex act was depicted in every conceivable form, performed by every combination of people, animals and inanimate objects. Ducks with shiny black bills did it with frogs and peanut men. One-eyed sea captains did it with motorcycle dykes. Star clusters did it with chrome spaceships and country bumpkins in gingham dresses did it with willing cows. Cops were depicted as uniformed swine with spiked clubs, wading into crowds of peace-loving flower children like Sherman wading into Georgia. Flakey Foont agonized over the cosmic duality of it all and was set straight by a slap across the chops from Mr. Natural.

Behind the counter lounged a shaggy man who guarded the smoking accessories. The rolling papers in every size, color and flavor, including jumbo-sized American-flag papers, saturated with essence of apple pie. The roach clips with their curling copper wire handles and leather and beaded decorations hanging down, the hash pipes and hookahs, the inlaid pill boxes and endless jewelry, created by overnight artists, in silver and gold, amber and turquoise and jade. Big beads, bells and earrings from India that made a lot of ethnic noise when you walked. Nose rings. Snake bracelets. Ankhs, peace symbols, slogan pins. Carved wooden hands that gave the perpetual finger to the perpetually deserving. Racks of incense. Frangipani and sandalwood hanging in the air like fog over the Ganges. Wind chimes that clanked and pinged and rang in the doorway. Signs on the wall admonishing shoplifters to remember their karma.

Many a tourist and weekend hippie took home a souvenir as proof of their visit to the Street of Love. A macrame belt, a copy of the Berkeley Barb or the Oracle, a tiny crumpled joint hidden away in the deepest recesses of their wallet – more well-hidden than the condom. Later they would bring it out, hold it as though it were a live grenade, and with trembling hands and a certainty that they were risking everything, they'd light up. The desire to get high has often trumped the fear of consequences.

Thanks to the media and an older generation of ultra-conservatives, everyone between the two coasts of America had been taught to fear the killer weed like it feared little else. Scare movies were shown to high school students, depicting marijuana as the "weed with roots in Hell", capable of turning clean-cut American kids into homicidal fiends overnight. Johnny, a "good boy" in the eyes of his poor, hard-working mother, had been bullied into trying the stuff – peer pressure in action. Not wishing to seem like a square, he took one tiny puff from a reefer, didn't even inhale, and immediately threw up his guts. Who could resist such a pleasurable experience? He was hooked from that moment forward.

Shaking and hollow-eyed from sleepless nights, he took to stealing from his boss at the grocery store to feed his ever-growing habit. In one especially true-to-life scene, Johnny and his pals, completely bombed out of their skulls and staggering down the street like three silent-movie drunks, got their kicks by breaking open Coke bottles and drinking from the jagged edges. Of course they cut their mouths off, but were so anesthetized by pot that they didn't feel a thing. The next obvious step is that Johnny starts shooting heroin almost immediately.

It was only a matter of time before Johnny wound up before a bespectacled judge after committing an unspeakable and demented act. Johnny was one of the lucky ones, though. The kindly old judge went easy on him, giving him one more chance to prove he could make something of himself and become a productive member of society. In the final scene, Johnny is seen wearing a tie and going to the school pep rally with the other honor students. All because he stopped smoking reefer.

This horror movie was shown alongside anti-cigarette films, in which smokers got their lungs yanked out in living Technicolor, and anti-drinking films, where drunk drivers wound up on slabs in the morgue, their brains eaten away by alcohol. The difference was, the smoking and drinking films *actually were* documentaries. Somehow, most people seemed to be OK with having lungs removed and brains eaten. At least they would die in a socially-acceptable way – conformist, government sanctioned, red-blooded Americans to the end.

Jimmy's eye landed on Sarah one night as she

bounced into the kitchen in search of a hot plate of brown rice and veggies. He looked up in silent curiosity from his newspaper and eyed her over the top of his ever-present eyeglasses, the thick spectacles which made him look like the perpetual reader he was. He spent his time attending classes at San Francisco State, reading every available anti-war article he could find, attending peace rallies and marches and sit-ins on every campus in the Bay Area and secretly and quietly suffering the loneliness only a homely 24-year-old virgin with no sense of rhythm can. He tried to play an old guitar, but it was by necessity a solo pursuit because the talented musicians at Cole Street, open-minded as they were, could not find a way to incorporate his failed attempts at song into their nightly sessions. It was just embarrassing. So Jimmy banged away in his room, unable to even master the basic concept of keeping a beat. Sometimes he would put down his guitar, push his glasses up on his nose, stare out the window at the gray sky and feel himself becoming invisible.

Sarah bounded into the living room momentarily, just to see who was there, spotted

Tim and cheerfully said, "Oh – hi!"

She paused to smile at him, he opened his mouth uncertainly, then she turned on her heel and vanished back into the kitchen, completely unaware of the changes she had just put his brain through. He had taken in her wild blonde hair, years ahead of its time   in unstructured curliness, almost disappearing into the background with frizz, her face, not so much beautiful as it was cherubic and radiant with the blissful, childlike zest that was her perpetual state, her round, pink body under jeans and a flowing top. He allowed a long and intense gaze to rest on her retreating ass, his mouth still open, and marveled at the potential wonders one might find beneath those holey, stained jeans. He had sudden, intense visions of two pink mountains grinding against each other like the two halves of the San Andreas Fault, making the Earth move under the couch he was sitting on. She swept out of the room in a warm gust of patchouli oil, and he sat blinking at the space where she had been and sniffing the air.

It took him a week to get up the nerve to ask

her. A week of silent, squirming false starts and frustrating trips to his little room where he would bring out an ancient copy of Playboy, partly to remind himself that he could still function in that capacity, seeing Sarah's rolling ass before him, spending his lonely need quickly as he whispered her name, then dejectedly putting the magazine away under his thin, hard mattress. Jimmy had never been on a date. He had never even asked. Girls were a Pandora's box of angst – creatures who possessed unfathomable, pitch-black secrets he could never hope to approach. He watched, almost from the shadows, as they floated in and out of his sight, taking their mysteries with them, out of his reach forever. And he watched as *other* guys helped themselves to the shining, golden gifts which dripped from the very fingertips of these magic creatures. *Other* guys who knew how to talk to them and touch them and, sweet Jesus, have *sex* with them. He could hear it through the walls every night. Tom and Sheela. Patrick and Carla. An assortment of changing partners in other rooms. He would *never* be able to make a woman squeal like that.

One afternoon he made up his mind. He drank several cups of ginseng tea, took several deep breaths, and looked in the mirror. He took off his glasses. Aside from a few zits on his chin and a decided lack of hipness in his hairstyle, he found himself warming to his reflection. He turned to view the profile, and then back again.

"Hey, man," he whispered to the mirror, "You're not so goddamn horrible, after all."

And before the flush of self-esteem could wear off, he flung open his door and hurried down the hall.

Oh, shit! There she was! Bending over a steaming pot of rice in the kitchen. He stopped short in the doorway. His hand went to the back of his neck and he shot a helpless gaze down the dim hall toward the refuge of his room. A furious red color was creeping into his face and his heart throbbed with a sudden overload of adrenaline. Just as he was about to bolt, screaming, down the hallway, Sarah turned toward him and he was riveted to the spot.

"Oh, hi, Jimmy!" she gushed. "What's goin' on?"

And she stood there with a dripping spoon in her hand and smiled like the sun coming out.

"Um....." he said, groping desperately to remember her name, *his* name, what day it was, what city they were in and why he had come to the kitchen.

"Hey, you know what?" she went on cheerfully, "There's a movie at the Straight tonight – they're gonna show *Alice in Wonderland* – remember that one from when we were kids? It's *really* trippy!"

And she put the spoon back into the pot on the stove and stirred, still beaming happily at Jimmy.

"Yeah?" he said, his voice cracking at the end of the word.

"Well," she went on, "Do ya wanna see it? I

mean, we could go together?"

"Uh....." he choked.

"Great!" she said, beaming at him with her hand on her hip. And before his knees could buckle under him, he turned and ran to his room and slammed the door, only to yank it open again immediately to go back and ask her what time.

The bare floor of the Straight Theater was filled with dark shapes, silhouettes of headbanded hair, feathers, jacket fringe and the moving shadows of beaded roach clips smoking at one end. Alice was tripping her way through Wonderland on the screen, in much the same way her audience was tripping through the Haight after falling down a rabbit hole in Middle America. As she floated past bookshelves and china cupboards on her way to the bottom, the appreciative audience cheered for the psychedelicized mind of Lewis Carroll and the fabulous artists of the Disney studios, both many years ahead of their time. Sarah remembered all the Disney films – the first movies she had ever seen – as some of the best experiences of her life, with the ultimate masterpiece of animation, *Fantasia*, topping the list.

"Jeez," she whispered to Jimmy, passing a circulating joint to him, "they just don't make movies like *this* anymore!"

Jimmy took the roach clip from her hand and stared at it's glowing ash tip. He had never smoked pot before. He was afraid it would make him lose control. But as he gazed at the colors on the screen, smelled the perfume wafting from Sarah's warm body and felt a swelling inside his jeans, he decided tonight was the night. He put the roach to his lips and took a tiny puff. Sarah laughed.

"No, not like that.....you gotta *inhale*.....watch."

And she took the joint from him, pursed her lips and inhaled deeply, holding it in and handing it back and saying, "G'won, try it." with held breath.

Jimmy screwed up every ounce of courage and inhaled deeply, trying to keep it down. But, like all first-time pot smokers before him, he immediately began choking and gasping for breath and had to be patted on the back by sympathetic strangers around him.

"One more," said Sarah as soon as Jimmy had regained normal breathing.

"I dunno....." he said, reluctant to resume choking.

But she held the burning roach up to his mouth, and smiled into his eyes and he was a goner. The choking wasn't quite as bad this time, and someone handed him a bottle of apple juice to drink from, and by the time he had passed it back and wiped his mouth, he was beginning to notice an entirely new feeling. Could it be? Yes, it could. Jimmy was getting high.

Sarah was becoming more beautiful somehow, although she hadn't changed. The glow from the movie screen was reflecting its colored lights onto her smooth cheeks and he had to resist the impulse to stroke her skin to see if he could feel the colors there. He noticed all the faces around him turned toward the screen, too, and they were all laughing. As he stared, the thought came to him that he couldn't tell which faces were male and which were female and that, furthermore, although some habitual internal mechanism tried to tell him he should be concerned about this, he found himself not caring at all. In fact, he began to formulate a theory that not only did it not matter, but that there was in fact *no difference* between male and female, and that all his previous angst about the mystery of women had been a colossal waste of time and energy. He gazed at Sarah lovingly, and, feeling his gaze, she turned and smiled beatifically, sending his heart into love-throbs. She laughed, evidently reading his mind, and kissed him quickly, still laughing. Eyes wide, he turned back to the movie and marveled.

"Jimmy," he said to himself, "You dog, you. You're actually gonna get laid!"

18 LOVE THE ONE YOU'RE WITH

Please then remember and don't get too close
To one special one – he will take your defenses and
run
Time to change partners
Again

Change Partners
Steven Stills

Rose was on summer vacation. She'd heard about the Haight back in Philadelphia, the same way thousands of others had, and she took off from home armed with just the information that it was the coolest place in the world and that it was located in San Francisco. Rose had cousins living in Marin County, north of the City, and came to stay with them. Her best friend from high school, Rita, was already living in the flat on Cole Street – sharing a room with her cousin Bernie. Rose didn't realize how far she'd have to travel to get back and forth from San Rafael to San Francisco, and she couldn't drive and her cousin, Eddie, had to use his only car to go to work. So Rose was stuck at the house most of the time, watching TV and pining for the action she was sure she was missing out on.

Eddie had his eye on Rose's 17-year-old body, but he couldn't figure out how to deflower her without everybody, including his wife, finding out. She was petite and thin, with short, black hair and big eyes, giving her a mod, elfin, American-Bandstand-regular look, and with a cigarette between her fingers and her miniskirt up around her ass, she was just Eddie's cup of tea. He watched her out of the corner of his eye and grumbled in frustration. He wouldn't take her to the City – he wanted her around the house. Rose began to feel uneasy in his presence.

She finally got up enough nerve to hitchhike. Rita had told her that everybody did it out here. Everyone was really nonviolent. Nobody would bother her. So she stuck out her thumb on Highway 101 and got a ride immediately with three guys in a big van who shared a joint with her in the back. The three of them all wanted to get it on with her, but she told them she was saving it for Mister Right. She'd know him when she saw him.

She saw him in Provo Park. Tom was in Berkeley with his friends, Don and Laura, sitting on the grass, watching the girls go by and listening to the music that was always free in the parks. Rose had met Rita and Bernie there – later there was supposed to be a "happening", with anti-war speeches and live bands. She was eating it up like layer cake – it was like San Francisco, only more authentic, more grass-roots and full of dedicated student activists. There were no "weekend" hippies here. These people were hardcore 24 hours a day and looked like they'd been at it for years. The music was loud, the people were dancing and Rose was in the middle of it all, going with the flow. In Philadelphia they had dances with steps. There were no recognizable patterns here – it was all free-form, no inhibition, no shame. This must have been what they meant by letting it all hang out. She plunged into it with the energy of the recently-liberated, tasting real freedom for the first time and loving every minute of it.

She caught Tom's eye and he caught hers. He was talking to Rita and Bernie, who had just bumped into the group sitting on the grass. They were laughing at the coincidence as Rose ran toward them. Tom didn't know it, but she had just seen the man of her dreams and it was him. She flung herself at him, almost knocking him over, while everyone watched, open-mouthed and laughing with surprise. Who was this? What was she doing? Rose barely knew herself, but she had to have this man!

Tom and his friends left almost immediately, laughing in embarrassment and looking back at Rose, wondering what the hell had just happened. And though he tried to forget all about it, he spent the next few days thinking about this sweet, young girl with her black eyes and pink lipstick and miniskirt. And the other women in his life – Sheela and Carla and perhaps one or two more – took a back seat in his thoughts.

Bernie met Rose at the I and Thou coffeehouse on Haight Street for some hot cider. He was lusting after her, like every other guy, but his hopes were quickly dashed when she started raving about Tommy, as she called him, and how outta sight he was and how she wanted him. Bernie listened dejectedly as she went on about how she had had a vision of the perfect man for her, and how, when she saw Tommy, that vision became a mind-blowing reality. She wanted him more than anything.

"And what about Sheela and the kids?" said Bernie.

"And what about Rita?" said Rose.

Bernie tried to look innocent, but couldn't keep from smiling at Rose's perceptive remark.

"Well, you know," he said, we're not married or anything – and besides, haven't you heard of Free Love? It's all about cutting loose from the old possessiveness of marriage and seeing if maybe some other arrangement works better. You're beautiful! I'm human, after all!"

Rose just laughed. "All I know is I"m saving myself for the right man, and it's him. Sorry."

Bernie shook his head and wiped some cider

from his black, curly mustache. After a while he said,

"Don't tell Rita, OK?"

Rose did everything she could think of to get Tom to cure her virginity. But in spite of a definite interest on his part, he stopped himself in time to wish her an almost platonic farewell when she left, broken-hearted, for Philadelphia and her final year of school.

Almost immediately, Tom began receiving thick letters from her, full of protracted, soulful confessions of love for him. Carla shook her head incredulously as he read one of them to her in the hall at Cole Street one morning.

"I don't believe you, Tom! What does this girl mean to you, anyway?" Tom shook his head helplessly, frowning and smiling at the same time, waving the pages of the letter in his hands.

"She don't mean nothin' to me – I mean, I don't know anything about her – she jumped all over me the first time I ever saw her – I'm tellin' ya, she don't mean *nothin'.*"

Carla gave him a look.

"Well, all I can say is, this kid's hooked, and if you cop her cherry, you're gonna be stuck with her forever."

"I ain't gonna screw her!" he said. "I'm just gonna drive across the country with Bernie because we've never done it and we wanna see what it's like. I don't have any intention....."

"Right," said Carla, and walked down the hall to the kitchen.

A few weeks later, Tom and Bernie left for their cross-country drive. Carla watched them go from the window, with Scruffy by her side. *He's full of shit*, she thought.

For the three weeks they were gone, Scruffy followed Carla from room to room like an orphan of the wars. He lay on the bathroom floor and gazed mournfully up at her with dewy eyes as she tried to bathe in peace. He slept outside the door of her room at night, so that she tripped over his big carcass every morning on her way to the bathroom. He spent the night thumping the floor, scratching his fleas, snoring and slurping at himself until Carla wanted to scream. He looked her in the eye, knowing she had the clue to Tom's whereabouts. He whined pitifully. He lay dejected. He waited.

They all had to bite their tongues when Tom came tromping up the stairs one afternoon, his bags in his hands, his hair and beard longer, looking weary but happy. They all wanted to blurt out the obvious question: *Did you screw her???*

Sheela looked both happy and sad to see him, and Carla could hear her later that night squealing as she and Tom made love in the next room. She had given up on the idea of a romantic relationship with Tom almost from the start. The conditions weren't right for it then, and looked even less so now – now that he'd been with Rose. He didn't have to tell her. She could tell that he hadn't been able to resist. Besides, Carla was pregnant and married and changing all that right then would have been just too much psychodrama. Tom was not only out of her hands, but soon to be out of Sheela's, too.

Carla and Patrick moved into the apartment directly below Tom & Sheela's, and Carla gave birth to a baby girl on Sheela's birthday. They named her Darcy, after the heroine of Ian & Sylvia's sad folk song, "Darcy Farrow". It was spring and life was sweet.

Tom may or may not have confessed the real extent of his relationship with Rose to Sheela, but they all found out the truth when Rose showed up with a suitcase in each hand and a huge smile on her face. She moved into the Cole Street apartment. Carla didn't even want to know how that arrangement was worked out among them. She was busy taking care of the baby and, although she couldn't say for sure how it started, she began receiving weekly visits from Brandon.

In his moments of open-mindedness Patrick espoused non-possessive love as the only way, especially since it had to work both ways to work at all. He wasted little time taking advantage of the freedom that had automatically become his upon learning of Carla's infidelity. He left her at home, slept with the first woman who made herself available, and discovered the joys of promiscuity on his own.

Julie would walk into a room and immediately spot the men who would be willing to have sex with her before the night was over. She managed to get nine out of ten correctly. Married or otherwise. And Patrick slept with her the first time they saw each other. She just moved right in on him and he didn't even put up a fight. She was a nymphomaniac, after all, and what man could resist? Patrick took to sleeping with her after party nights while Carla was home with the baby. He wouldn't bother to tell her he wasn't coming home in the morning – that would have been too much like a straight, uptight, possessive marriage.

All the women at the Cole Street apartment who had seen Julie in action wanted to wring her neck. But they got sweet revenge when the story spread through the building that she had tried to cure Larry of his virginity and he *couldn't get it up*. Evidently, there was at least one guy who found her too aggressive – one guy she couldn't have. All the women loved Larry after that.

Brandon had visited Tom on Cole Street a few times – he liked to smoke some pot and listen to home-grown music, and one night he had seen Carla and asked Tom about her. Tom was a little taken aback. Brandon was married to Donna, had a 3-year-old boy with her, but they were separated, and he had moved a tall, aspiring model into his house whom the women at Cole Street snidely referred to as The Amazon.

Tom stared at Brandon. "Carla's great, but she's married to Patrick and they have a little baby....."

Brandon just nodded, smiling.

Tom stroked his beard uncertainly. Even though he was no longer intimate with Carla, he felt a small pang of jealousy.

"Anyway," Tom said, "she lives downstairs."

He shrugged. He didn't want to give Brandon any ideas. He shrugged again and got up to turn the record over.

Brandon rang Carla's doorbell a week later, in the morning when Patrick was at work. He came up the stairs slowly, smiling, and Carla found herself immediately sensing *why* he was there. *Oh, God!* She thought. *Here we go again.*

The two of them walked the streets of the Haight, pushing the stroller, eating ice cream, getting to know each other, all that early summer.

Patrick was off doing his own thing with other women, and Carla was learning to lean on Brandon for just about everything. One day he said to her that if she ever found herself without a home, that he would take care of her. That time came soon enough, when she confronted Patrick about their future together. She asked him if he even wanted to be her husband or Darcy's father anymore, and he told her no. Then he went off to play music and drink with his friends, while Carla cried half the night on Tom's shoulder. Sheela had left Tom after Rose moved in, taking the kids and following a guru to the East Coast. Tom told Carla as she sobbed that he loved her, and that he always would. She had heard those words from her parents, who abused her. She had heard them from high school boys, who just wanted sex. She had heard them from Patrick, who changed his mind once he had a few girlfriends on the side. She had heard them and now wondered what they meant. But Tom's simple declaration rang true, because he didn't say it out of obligation or as a means to an end and he said it in spite of the fact he had numerous women before, during and after his affair with Carla. She was crying in his arms over another man, he was with another woman. They would never marry each other, live together or have children together. They would go decades without seeing each other. But even as he drew near the end of his life, Tom kept his word. And Carla's heart was broken, in the best of ways, every time he told her he loved her, which was every time he spoke to her.

She packed up the baby's crib and went with

Brandon to live on his boat in Redwood City. They couldn't live in his house, because The Amazon was still there. She never lived in the Haight again. She only returned, a year later, to help Tom, Rose and their new baby move out of the apartment on Cole Street, out of the City and back to the land.

19 WE CAN WORK IT OUT

We love each other – it's plain to see
There's just one answer that comes to me
Sister-lovers, water brothers, and in time – maybe
others
So you see – what we can do is to try something
new, if you're crazy too
I don't really see – why can't we go on as three

Triad
David Crosby

One Sunday afternoon when the fog was held behind the Golden Gate by a pale yellow sun, Harry bought four tabs of LSD from a guy on Stanyan Street and brought them home to share. He told himself as he climbed the stairs it would be with the first three people he saw in the flat. Turning right at the top of the steps and peeling off his old denim jacket, he strode into the hazy kitchen and saw Rose, Tom and Sheela sitting around the table, smoking Marlboros and greeting him with smiles. He threw himself into the chair across from Rose and dug into his shirt pocket.

"Guess what I've got for you guys!" he said. His blue eyes twinkled.

Rose turned her hand upwards. "Don't keep us in suspense....."

They smoked in silence while Harry unraveled the baggie containing four tiny squares of paper, each with a blue dot in the center.

"Holy shit," said Sheela, leaning in to get a closer look. "Is that what I think it is?"

"Absolutely," said Harry, and he promptly placed one tab in front of the other three leaving one for himself. Then he got up and got a bottle of apple juice from the fridge and brought it back and sat down. He grinned at the other three, who smiled, open-mouthed, at each other then at him.

"Allow me to demonstrate," he said.

He licked his forefinger, placed it on the acid tab, lifted the tab to his tongue, then took a long swig of apple juice and held the bottle out to

Sheela.

"Well I guess we're doing this!" Sheela said, and followed his example. She shook her head, laughing and stubbing out her cigarette.

Tom chuckled and said, "Oh man. Here we go again, huh?"

Rose gave everyone a questioning smile, stared at the tab on her fingertip, said, "Oh my god." and swallowed it, dribbling some juice down her chin and wiping it away with her fingers. The four of them said nothing for a few seconds then burst into hysterical giggling at the prospect of the trip that lay before them.

Harry had a little camera and wanted to take some pictures. He suggested they all go to the beach, since it was such a sunny day. They were heading down the stairs, with Scruffy leading the way, when Patrick and Carla opened the front door.

"Hey!" said Patrick. "Where you guys goin"?"

Sheela put her arm through Patrick's and said, "C'mon, we're goin' to the beach, and you're driving."

"OK," said Patrick. "Uh.....why am I driving?"

"Because we all just dropped acid," said Rose, shepherding everyone out the door and down the front steps.

"No shit?" said Patrick. "Didn't you leave any for me?"

"Sorry," said Harry. "It was in the hands of the gods....."

Patrick just looked at him with a knowing smile and went around the front of Tom's old Chevy to get in the driver's seat. Carla was glad she hadn't been one of the chosen. Her one experience with LSD was enough. Anxiety-prone and empathic by nature, it was enough for her to just be with others who were on acid. She always got a nervous contact high at the beginning of the trip, and was glad when she could go to bed and fall asleep and feel like the "normal" one in the group.

They drove through Golden Gate Park, past the ornate, white, glassed-in conservatory with tourists sprinkled over its manicured grounds, past the fields of lawn bordered with Eucalyptus, giant ferns, rhododendrons and pale hydrangea flowers, past the rear of the DeYoung Museum, the Japanese Tea Garden, past the polo grounds and Stow Lake, where white swans floated on black water, past the giant windmill and out to Ocean Beach, where whitecaps drove across the blue-gray shoreline. Patrick parked the car in front of the concrete sea wall, and they all climbed out of the car and down the steps to the cold sand, where they took off their shoes and looked around. Sheela had a blanket, which they spread on the sand and plopped down on, lying on their stomachs, facing inward, smiling at each other expectantly. Carla lay with her head against Tom's calves, looking at the racing clouds overhead. Rose lit another cigarette, as Harry held his jacket out from his side as a shield against the wind. She took a deep drag and stared at Tom. Sheela played with the fringe on someone's leather jacket. Tom leaned on one elbow, slapping his thigh softly and grinning.

Harry turned to squint into the lowering sun. "What are we doing?" he said quietly.

Carla looked into his eyes and said nothing. She got a little knot in her stomach. She knew what was coming.

"We're sittin' at the beach, havin' fun," said Tom, slapping his thigh again.

"We're just trying to figure things out," said Sheela. She knew what Harry meant. She stroked his arm protectively. He turned and gazed at her for a long time.

Patrick sat up and crossed his legs. "I dunno how the rest of you all feel about it, but I really feel like we *belong* here. I never felt like that before." He toyed with some fuzz on the blanket. "Ya know? I mean, maybe it won't be like this forever, but at least we have it *now,* and at least we have each other."

"Damn straight." said Tom.

Harry jumped to his feet in a sudden burst of energy. "Hey, let's take some pictures!" he grabbed the camera from the center of the blanket and began to move around them in a circle, squinting through the viewfinder and snapping shots from every angle, giggling to himself and shouting out directions against the strong wind. The conversation was getting more animated. Tom was talking about money. He took a dollar bill out of his wallet and crumpled it up in his hands, chuckling.

"What's a dollar bill?" he said, staring hard at the ball in his hand. "It's this piece of paper! You can't eat it. It's not big enough to use as a blanket to cover yourself at night....."

"Unless you got really, really *small*....." said Sheela. And she plucked the bill from Tom's hand gingerly and pictured herself as a Thumbelina-sized Sheela, sleeping, hands folded under her cheek, beneath this enormous engraving of George Washington.

"Well, you trade it for stuff you *can* eat," said Patrick. "That's really all it is. Trouble is, it's become *everything* to most people. The be-all and the end-all. Something about that's gotta change. We need to have other reasons to be alive....."

"Look at us," said Carla. "We're getting by on practically *no* money – it's because we're willing to *share*. They told us to share, didn't they? So now we're doing it! Bet they didn't expect us to share *everything!*"

"Yeah.....*everything*....." said Sheela, glancing from Carla to Rose to Tom.

Rose buried her head between her knees. "Oh God," she said.

"Hey," said Sheela, reaching over to touch Rose's bare foot. "It's OK! Really! I'm not exactly guilt-free in all this, you know. We all just wanted to see what it was like to be free.....didn't we?"

Rose rolled her head back and forth. "I'm too fucking high," she said.

Harry got up and grabbed Rose under the armpits and pulled her to her feet.

"Let's go see how cold the water is!"

"No colder than the Arctic Ocean," said Carla, as the two ran toward the breaking surf. "Tell me you're not all going skinny-dipping," she added.

"Are you kidding?" said Tom. "Those tourists over there would call the cops for sure! Don't you know a naked body is a sin and a crime? What would happen if some little kid saw somebody naked? The world would stop spinning!"

Rose and Harry were pulling each other around in circles, trying to throw each other into the frigid surf, and laughing their heads off. Patrick lay down on his back, and Sheela began brushing his hair with her fingers. She was humming and slowly rocking, and she gradually began to sing, putting her head back and closing her eyes.

"As I went walking that ribbon of highway, I saw above me that endless skyway....."

Patrick and Carla joined in the well-known Woody Guthrie song, harmonizing and clapping their hands. Tom couldn't sing, but he couldn't wipe the smile off his face, either. Life was beyond good at this moment. He was surrounded by women he loved, even men he loved, and they were singing in angels' voices and the air was turning rainbow colors and he could see the blood flowing through the veins in his hands and the sand was like sparkling sugar and the waves were literally caressing the shore with tender blue fingers.

"Oh, man!" was all he could say, and he fell back laughing.

Rose and Harry came running back, still holding hands. "You gotta see these *fish*," said Rose. "They were jumping at us, trying to get in our pockets!"

Harry fell into the middle of the blanket and stared up at the darkening sky. He could feel the Earth rotating under him, its massive form grinding, roaring, pulling him toward its center, but gently floating him on its sandy surface at the same time.

He reached for the nearest hand, and it was Patrick's. It didn't matter. He held it anyway.

Sheela stood up and said, "It's time to go home and get warm and play some music!"

Without hesitation, they all got to their feet, Patrick pulling Harry up by the hand he was still holding. They hurried toward the car, suddenly shivering with cold.

As Patrick drove slowly through the park and then into the Haight, Harry and Sheela and Rose cuddled in the back while Tom pointed out the streetlights and signs lining the urban pavements, marveling at their brilliant shapes and colors.

After they had taken off their jackets and lit cigarettes and had some hot tea, Patrick brought out his Martin guitar and his book of songs, and started strumming the chords to *Four Strong Winds* by Ian Tyson. Carla immediately started singing the melody and Patrick and Sheela harmonized while Rose swayed back and forth, hugging herself and smiling. She began to cry at the vision the song brought to mind – a lonely cowboy out on the plains, a woman he couldn't expect to stay, and the heartbreaking chorus, which they sang over and over,

> *Four strong winds that blow lonely*
> *Seven seas that run high*
> *All those things that don't change, come what may*
> *But our good times are all gone*
> *And I'm bound for movin' on*
> *I'll look for you if I'm ever back this way*

Tom put his arm around her shoulder. The singing changed from one song to the next, but they were all slow and sad and beautiful. Patrick put down his guitar at last and leaned back on the couch. They were silent for a long time, staring at the candles which were on a table in a corner. Someone had turned the lights out, or maybe they had never been turned on, and they sat in the dark, with only the dancing candle flames.

"I love you guys," Harry said.

"Me, too," said Sheela.

They found themselves sitting on the floor in a circle, holding hands.

"I wish we could just go off somewhere together," said Patrick.

"Hey, we *can*," said Tom. "Why don't we all build a boat together, then we can take off in it."

"Tom.....Sheela groaned.

"How would that even *work*? said Harry. "I mean – you and Sheela and Rose? And *me* and Sheela and Rose? And you and Carla, and Patrick and Carla, and who-knows-who else? What are we doing? This is dumb! We're just a bunch of kids – we're experimenting, we're playacting, wearing costumes – this ain't gonna work."

"Hey," said Sheela, "it's not all about sex. It doesn't just boil down to who's sleeping with who – it's about learning a different way – a better way than what we were taught. Look at all the people who get married and go by the rules and then wind up divorced anyway. How are we any worse than them? At least we love each other. Rose and Carla and I could have hated each other, but instead we're friends. How is that a bad thing?"

Carla looked over at Rose and Rose looked over at Sheela. Sheela winked at Rose. Rose blew a kiss to Carla. Patrick, taking a long pull on a freshly-rolled joint, smiled blissfully. Tom wanted to take them all in his arms forever.

"It can't last," Harry said. "You'll see. Twenty years from now we'll all be married and living just like everybody else – one couple in every house. Communal living doesn't work. Eventually, we all pair off. It's *natural*. It's human nature."

"So is violence and war. Doesn't make it right," said Carla.

"And racial prejudice. And treating women like shit. And religious fanaticism," said Sheela. "They've all been around forever. Don't make `em right."

"Yeah, but *monogamy*. I mean, come on. You

know we're all gonna wind up with just one person. Jealousy ruins everything.....”

"What about the Haskin family?" said Patrick. "They all got married to each other and they're making it work....."

"Yeah, but when they got married they stayed up all night trying to figure out who was gonna sleep with who and in the end they wound up in bed with their original partners because they thought anything else would be too, you know, uncomfortable. Right off the bat, they're having possessiveness and jealousy problems. It just can't *last.*"

'We'll see," said Sheela, getting up and stretching. "Right now I need some *hot chocolate!*"

There was general agreement all around that cocoa was indeed the next logical step. Carla went to bed. Everyone else stayed up most of the night, tearing the world apart, then putting it carefully back together again, new and improved.

And we'll go dancing, Baby, then you'll see
How the magic's in the music
And the music's in me

Do You Believe in Magic
John Sebastian

Blossom grabbed the microphone, took a deep breath, and screamed out the first line of the song. When she dared to open her eyes, she saw a packed mob jumping up and down in time to the music, glittering and blurring in the bright afternoon sunshine. The colors and swaying and the screeching feedback from Mike's guitar made her squeeze them shut again. The pot she'd smoked with the band, down on the street a few minutes ago, let her open up her throat and find the impossible notes and bend them around like Janis would – or so she hoped. It *felt* right, it *sounded* right – she was exactly where she wanted to be at last. They were set up on a flatbed truck parked in front of the Straight Theater, surrounded by a sea of heads stretching five blocks down Haight Street and spilling into the side streets. Enormous speakers took up half the space and the band had to squeeze together, stepping over fat cables and trying to avoid poking each other with their guitar heads. Ramon, the drummer, just closed his eyes in concentration and went for it, grimacing and smiling at the same time. His long, black curly hair dripped with sweat which flew off in great arcs as he shook his head over his drum set. Carla was squeezed in behind him. They had said she could play the tambourine and cowbell at the street gig. Since they weren't getting paid, it was no big deal if she missed a beat or two. She didn't, though. They joked with her that she had great rhythm.....for a White girl.

Blossom and Carla had joined in during garage rehearsals with the group, named *Head Band* by Mike late one night after tripping on acid and having a vision of fame and fortune. Everyone in the band wanted fame, wanted to stand on a stage and hear that applause, wanted to be Jimi and Janis and the Stones and see their posters on everyone's wall – everyone but Carla. She loved to sing, but felt better at the back of the stage than at the front. But Blossom thrived in the spotlight. Her family had been loud and raucous and every meal was a political and social rally and noisy restaurant combined. She grew up clamoring for, and getting, attention, and she loved it. Her singing voice was strong and arresting – a natural lead. When she and Carla harmonized, Blossom took the high melody and Carla the lower harmony. Although Carla could carry a tune well, her range was small and her low self-confidence prevented her from letting it burst out.

She had a very limited ability to play guitar and piano, and could keep up in a rhythm capacity, but could never do any kind of a solo. Practicing with the guys was one of the best experiences of her young life. They had just enough collective talent to pull off a decent cover of an easy song, but could only dream about making it big. Carla was thrilled when the guys "allowed" her to play piano on a couple of songs, and one of them told her she was better than their regular keyboard player. Thrilled, but unconvinced. She thought the regular guy must have been pretty bad. She had never learned to read or write music. Her knowledge was limited to a book of guitar chords and a few sessions with her high school boyfriend who taught her the basic, 3-finger piano chords. She never rose beyond *almost* good. But here she was, and for the moment, it was better than drugs.

Music was at the center of everything, all around the perimeter, booming up from the Earth, glittering down from the sky – it was inconceivable to go through a day without it. There was a melody and a lyric for every feeling it was possible to have – it had all been said – but they never tired of hearing new methods of expressing their same shared experiences, and never stopped trying to create their own new songs. Music filled a palpable need nothing else could touch. After work was done for the day, after love was made, after the dishes were washed and put away and after the pipe was filled and passed around – there was still one more thing to do, and that was to make music.

Mike lived with the other band members in an apartment above a Mexican bakery in the Mission District. The place had been christened the "Heartbreak Hotel" by Rene, who was Ramon's cousin – a gorgeous bass player with a passive, mellow personality. He had been married to Cassie, and they had a little boy, but Cassie had left with another guy, and Rene stayed with the band – all single guys, most of them nursing broken hearts, between women, dreaming of groupies, but living for music above all else. They got up in the middle of the day, threw together what they could find in the little kitchen, picked up their instruments, lit joints, slouched on the dusty old sofa and picked out tunes, experimenting with instrumental breaks.

Blossom and Carla would show up sometimes in the late afternoon, wearing their Indian kurtas, beads and essential oils, ready for a chance to sing with the guys and hopefully wiggle their way into their hearts. Blossom and Ramon couldn't keep their eyes off each other, and after hours, couldn't keep their hands off, either. Carla and Rene became a couple for a while, beginning the night the four of them took Mescaline and went to a restaurant in Chinatown. By the time their order arrived, they were all too wired to eat a bite, and they had the befuddled waiters put the whole meal into takeout cartons so they could just *get outside into the air.* After rushing around the Chinatown streets for a while, they caught a bus back to the apartment and threw off their coats and had something to drink. The four of them wound up on Carla's bed, giving each other back massages to help slow them down.

Ramon and Blossom soon disappeared into Blossom's bedroom, and Carla closed the door behind them, after seeing that they were already making mad love. She and Rene kissed, but he said he was "too nervous" to do anything else, and soon left for home.

They spent a lot of time with each other after that, but when they talked about moving in together, it was Carla who felt it wasn't a good idea. He was a rocker, staying up all night and sleeping half the day, and she had her little girl to take care of and kept more regular hours. They drifted apart, and he shortly left for New York City to play in a bigger, more fame-oriented band and did well for a few years before hard drugs, infighting and jealousy broke the group apart.

Heartbreak Hotel was still open for business, and Rene went back to its lonely rooms.

The band had regrouped, taken on new members, including Mike, who became lead guitarist by default – he was a fair musician, but his true talent lay in his art. He had a cartoon style of drawing and painting, with a contemporary political commentary running throughout. Tony and Ricky both played rhythm guitar, Ramon was the percussionist, Eduardo was the Keyboardist and Rene played bass. There were always hangers-on and a few groupies in and out of Heartbreak Hotel, and the air was always thick with smoke and booming jam sessions. The neighbors complained on a regular basis, but Rene would smile sweetly and shrug and apologize, and then go pick up his bass again.

Blossom was now belting out the end of the song, and Mike was eyeing his playlist, taped to the back of his guitar. He decided they'd close with a song which had become kind of the band's mascot – just for the hell of it. He turned and motioned to Carla with his head to get up to the front of the stage. He mouthed the words, "What's Your Name" and Carla's heart jumped. *Holy shit! she thought.*

She grabbed Ramon's beer bottle, which was sitting on one of the drum cases behind him, and took a long swig of the sun-warmed brew. Then, as the crowd applauded and cheered, she made her way to Blossom's side.

"Oh my GOD!" said Blossom. "Are we ready?"

"I guess we *have* to be!" said Carla, gritting her teeth and stepping up to the microphone. They looked over at Mike, who had a lazy smile on his face as he nodded to Ramon, then to the two of them. Ramon counted off,

"Dos, tres, quatro....."

And everyone came in, more or less on cue, with the standard rock-ballad, four-chord progression, while the audience cheered, then paired off to do a little slow dancing in front of the flatbed. After two bars, Blossom and Carla, the former high and the latter low, came in with the old lyrics to a well-loved song form their teen years, *"What's Your Name"* by Don and Juan.

"What's your name, I have seen you before
What's your name, may I walk you to your door...."

The guys were hamming it up on their guitars, and Mike was doing his best to throw in the appropriate riffs in the appropriate spaces. It didn't take long to get to the bridge, and when Blossom took the high solo, Mike went crazy backing her up with psychedelic do-wop on his electric guitar. Carla and Blossom could barely stifle their laughter trying to finish the song, but by this point it didn't matter – the audience would have cheered them regardless. They finished with a drum flourish from the exhausted Ramon, and climbed down from the truck, sweaty and happy. Blossom had a taste of the limelight and was ready for more. Carla was feeling good, mainly from relief, but stage fright kept her in the background from then on.

Blossom and Ramon got married and moved to a different part of the City, and they each had their day jobs.   Music was at night and on weekends. But *every* night and *every* weekend.

Head Band morphed into several different configurations, members came and went, and they never stuck with a core group or a trademark sound long enough to become known and popular. Eventually, everyone had to get a job, a woman, and a home.

Carla still has a single, time-worn and faded-almost-to-white photo she took of the group during their last incarnation, doing rhythm & blues covers, writing a few of their own, getting a few local gigs. The four remaining members are lined up in barbershop chairs, wearing leather jackets, wild hair, and looking old ahead of their time.

21 THE DARK END OF THE STREET

Take me to the station
And put me on a train
I've got no expectations
To pass through here again

No Expectations
Mick Jagger, Keith Richards

Karen from Bakersfield was listlessly packing her clothes into her battered old suitcase, getting ready to go back to her parents' suburban ranch house and start college. Roger had split with some other girl weeks ago, the job she had at the corner clothing store, Avant Garb, hadn't earned her enough to even pay the rent, and she had just enough saved for a bus ticket back.

She wouldn't tell her parents about the miscarriage she had suffered in August, bleeding onto the cold bathroom floor alone, seeing her tiny embryo disappear down the toilet and crying for three days before finally emerging with a new hard shell around her heart. She felt nothing now but emptiness mixed with a strange, small sense of guilty relief that she had not had to face the future as a single mother – that nature had intervened and she'd be better off for it. She would start all over again. Someday – not today, but someday – she'd be able to find another man, get married and have another child. For now, it was enough to take a last look around the bare little room, lock the memory away, and close the door behind her.

Rita and Bernie were saying goodbye on the stone steps of the commune Rita shared with six others just outside the Haight. Bernie was leaving for the Napa Valley, where he'd found a quiet little wood house on a back street and an internship at a local hospital. He would go on to become a doctor, serious as hell in his ponytail and sandals, prescribing medical marijuana to half the valley. The other half, of course, would prefer wine.

Rita wrapped her sweater more tightly around her shoulders as she watched her cousin drive away. They had loved each other deeply, but knew they couldn't be a family. Their fathers were brothers. That part alone was enough to make it impossible, if not immoral, but Rita didn't want kids and Bernie did, and that wouldn't change. Her face was dark as she climbed the stairs, re-living the incident of a few weeks before which had changed her feelings about a lot of things forever, although she didn't tell Bernie about it – only Rose. Rose was like a sister to her. They had been in high school together, had come to California during the same time and for the same reasons, and told each other everything.

Rita had been on the sidewalk in front of the Straight Theater that night, talking to Barbie and Steve, smoking a little pot, getting ready to walk back to the apartment. It was just getting dark and the fog was blowing in fast. She turned around and two young Black guys were standing there, and one of them just looked at her with deadened eyes and said,

"Gimme a kiss."

She almost laughed, but then thought better of it. Barbie and Steve were pretending they hadn't heard. Before she had time to respond, the kid leaned in and kissed her with a wet mouth. His breath was sour from drinking and she backed away, looking at Steve for a clue. Steve took a step forward with an upturned palm.

"Hey, man....." he said, smiling uncomfortably.

The kid turned his head but said nothing. Steve's smile evaporated. Suddenly two men appeared behind the black kids, and one of them was Ashton Bright, the guy with the megaphone in the park. He was wearing a knit scarf and corduroy jacket, looking like everyone's favorite college professor. He moved between the kid and Rita and stared at her, putting his hand to his bearded chin and asking her thoughtfully,

"Are you as pretty as I think you are?"

She could only stare back. She knew he was trying to rescue her, and for a minute, it worked. She took his arm and whispered,

"Walk me to the corner."

He nodded and smiled, and they headed down the sidewalk slowly, leaving the two kids and Ashton's friend with nothing to do but share the rest of the joint. Steve and Barbie hurried off toward the Cole Street flat. When Rita and Ash got to the corner, she looked back and saw that the guys didn't seem to be paying any attention, so she let go of his arm.

"Thanks," she said. "Those guys had *really* bad vibes. I live just a few blocks away....."

"No shit," Ash said. "Want me to take you home?"

"Oh, man, no thanks! It's OK, really.....it's just right up the street. Thanks again, that was really cool of you, thanks!"

And she took off, almost running, down the dark street. Ashton lit his pipe again and strolled back to meet is friend. The two kids got in their car, parked at a meter nearby, and sped away.

They turned right at the next corner, turned

right at the next, and saw Rita coming up the street toward them. They stopped the car, turned off the lights, and waited.

"When she came abreast of the car, they quickly jumped out and ran toward her. She leaped back in shock, looking around for some place to escape, tried to run up a nearby stoop, but they grabbed her, hard around the middle before she made the second step and yanked her back. She felt like she should scream, but nothing came out but air. Everything happened in a split second, and she was shoved into the back seat of the car and held down by the kid who had kissed her. He was breathing hard and she could smell his sour-stomach breath. It made her want to vomit. As the car sped away, she thought this was it. She was going to be murdered. All she could think of was how much she wished she and Bernie could stay together, how much she wished he weren't leaving. Maybe he could eventually get used to the idea of no kids. Maybe she would change her mind, maybe their parents would understand and.....

The kid holding her down suddenly said, "Pull

over, man!" And the car jerked to the right and stopped.

She heard the crunch of gravel or dirt under the wheels. She smelled the sharp tang of Eucalyptus through the half-open back window. They must be in the park, she thought. Then the kid told her to sit up. She slowly lifted her head and looked at him, and then at his partner in the front, who had his arm over the seat and was staring anxiously at her. She noticed his eyes. They seemed to be light in color. *How strange,* she thought.

Then it hit her. They were going to rape her, not murder her!

She switched from fear to rage in that instant. She looked from one to the other. They were both just teenagers – younger than she was – probably no more than fifteen or sixteen. They were clearly new at this, and were both nervous and sweating until their skin shone from the dim light across the way. She saw, over their shoulders, that they had pulled off to the side of the road in the park somewhere. There were no other cars around. She could see lights through the trees a few blocks away, but they were in a dark-colored car, under trees, on a foggy night and probably couldn't be seen by anyone. It was up to Rita to save herself.

Her rage overcame her fear. How *dare* these two assholes invade her life like this? What the hell gave them the right to take *anything* from her? At that moment, she didn't give a shit about their poverty, their broken homes, their disadvantages, their lack of education and positive role models and opportunity – *none of that* – she just wanted to bash their heads together and scream at them to *wise up!*

Instead, she quickly sat up and began to unbutton her blouse. The two boys shot a glance at each other and squirmed in their seats. What the fuck? Rita stopped and looked from one to the other in mock surprise.

"Well??" she said. "What are you waiting for?? Let's get it ON!"

The kid in back with her began to fumble uncertainly with his belt buckle. The kid in front gaped at them for a moment, then opened the door and got out, slamming it behind him and moving away from the car. He thrust his hands in his pockets and came out with a cigarette, which he lit with shaking hands.

Rita looked down and continued to unbutton, while the kid was still working on getting his belt undone.

"HURRY UP!" she yelled at him. "What's the matter? You don't wanna fuck me? You don't want some White pussy? Isn't that what this is all about? He just stared at her with his mouth open and his eyes completely confused. He couldn't figure out what to say or how this had gotten all turned around. Who *was* this chick, anyway?

"C'MON!" she said. "Let's GO! Get those pants off and let's see what you've got!"

She made a grab for his zipper, but he slapped her hand away like it was a snake about to bite.

"Fuck!" he growled. "You leave me alone, bitch!" He was backed up against the car door as far as he could go, and the sweat was standing on his face. Rita cocked her head questioningly and said,

"What's the matter? *Can't get it up?* Can't even get it up for *me?* I thought you wanted to fuck.....but maybe you don't even know *how!*" She was sneering now.

To her shock and relief, the kid suddenly opened the door, jumped out, backed off a few feet and yelled at her to get outta the car. Without hesitation, she scrambled across the seat and almost fell out the door, hugging the side of the car until she was standing behind it, forcing herself to hide her fear with a dark scowl.

The two boys huddled together for a quick, whispered conference, both glancing nervously at her and all around them. She thought of bolting, but she knew she could never outrun these guys.

She waited, her heart pounding out of her chest. WHY didn't another car drive by? What were they going to do to her now? Jesus, maybe they had guns or knives. The thought nearly made her knees collapse under her.

Finally, the two boys turned toward her. *This is really it now,* she thought. Before she had a chance to turn and run, the kid who had been driving said sharply,

"Just get the fuck outta here!"

The kid who had been in the back with her turned away and lit a cigarette as she was running into the trees. She heard the car doors slam and the engine start up as she stumbled across the wet grass of an open area in front of a slope. She heard the car disappearing fast into the distance as she scrambled up the slope and collapsed behind some wet shrubbery. She listened for a long time before she dared to stand up and look around. Then, pulling her clothes together and brushing herself off, she slowly and weakly started walking toward the lights from the nearest street. By the time she reached the sidewalk, she was shaking so much she simply sat down next to a streetlight, leaned against it and waited for this night to never have happened.

Sometime later, she stood up and started walking toward home. The streets were almost deserted, but as she passed a row of apartments near hers, a man in fringed leather and feathers, who was sitting on one of the stoops, playing a harmonica, stood up as she approached and smiled at her.

"Hey, Baby – you wanna ball?"

She didn't look up, but wrapped her coat around her more tightly, made a wide detour around him, and broke into a run.

"I guess not!", he said, and sat back down with his harmonica.

Scenes of my young years were warm in my mind
Visions of shadows that shined
`Til one day I returned, and found they were the
victims of the vines
Of changes

Changes
Phil Ochs

I get so tired, hangin' around this town
And this old city life can sure bring a fella down

Ba Di Da
Fred Neil

 Eatlemania, the cafe on the corner with an all-Beatles menu, was one of the last shops to fold. The owner, Mac, rubbing his balding head and frowning, said it was a real drag, but the neighborhood was going downhill. The restaurant had seemed like such a natural on a street full of loadies with the blind munchies. Tom and Carla had savored many an order of Babies in Black (baby lobster tails in black bean sauce) while Tom was still flush with his boat money. But now speedfreaks were coming in for a cup of coffee (Drank a Cup) and staying for hours, taking up table space, overfilling the ashtrays with cigarette butts and scaring away the tourists, the straights and the peacenik hippies.

"I can't even lock up at night without looking over my shoulder," he said. "There was a guy who got knifed by bikers just the other night, just because he accidentally bumped into a big Harley and knocked it over. Jesus. And my girls, my waitresses, are going back to where they came from or getting pregnant or turning tricks and who knows what. I saw Janie – best waitress I ever had when she first showed up. Real pretty, fun to be around. I kinda had a thing for her.....then she comes in the other day with some hard case. They looked like a couple a vampires.

"Speed! That fuckin' speed! I just don't get it – why does everyone wanna be all hyped up and paranoid? Whatever happened to just gettin' high and mellow on grass?" He shook his head, wiping the counter absently with his rag. "I'm thinkin' maybe I should try another line of work....."

And he gazed wearily out the front window, looking at the gray early-winter street, mostly deserted except for a handful of bundled-up panhandlers and a few longhaired girls trying to sell the *Berkeley Barb* on the corner. The Gray Line tour bus had discontinued its Haight-Ashbury run, so there were only the old city buses belching black smoke as they lumbered by. Pigeons fought over part of a Yellow Submarine Sandwich and some Onion Ringos someone had dropped in front of his door.

It was lunchtime and only one customer sat at a corner table having the special. He'd probably leave a quarter tip.

The daisies in a glass on top of the cash register were wilted and their petals fell onto the keys. Nobody noticed. Mac walked over to the door and flipped over the sign hanging from the handle.

"Open 8 Days a Week," he read to himself. "Not any more!"

The pond in the park at the Stanyan Street entrance was choked with litter. Cigarette butts, soda cans, shreds of paper bags, wine bottles. The grass all around was trampled and soggy, the park benches splintered and carved with graffiti. The sidewalks were full of broken bottles and oily black stains. Guys dressed in ragged army jackets and patched pants harassed every passer-by for spare change.

"Hey, Brother! Got a quarter? I'm hurtin'. How `bout a dime? C'mon, man! Help a brother out." – as they fell in step with people trying to avoid them. Some refused to make eye contact, some scowled angrily and shot back with retorts such as, "There's no such thing as `spare change'!" or "You're just gonna spend it on drugs!", both of which were basically true. But there was no way to win an argument with a panhandler. They had grown accustomed to the generous, flower-child attitude of the hippies, back when it was summer and love was thick in the air. Now pockets were empty and flower children were wilting.

Up in the apartment windows, Indian-bedspread curtains weren't so much in evidence and American flags had been taken down. More conventional draperies were drawn, or no curtains at all let the cold light into bare rooms. The front room at 625 Cole, where Carla and Patrick had once slept, was now empty except for a few orange crates they had used for beside tables. Carla was living with Brandon and Patrick had taken off for the Northwest again.

Tom and Rose were down the hall in the kitchen, packing dishes into cardboard boxes, cleaning out the pantry of its last few cans of tuna, smoking cigarettes and talking about the new place and the new life they were headed for. The weak light from the window fell across the rickety wooden table which had seen so many group meals of brown rice and steamed veggies.....there were dark rings where the bottle of soy sauce had sat.

The table would be one of the last things to go into the U-Haul trailer they rented for the trip up north. It wouldn't be long now. Tom had heard from one of Sheela's cousins about Humboldt County and the cheap land to be had – land where you could build a house, raise a family and grow your own food. Organic food, without all the poison pesticides and fertilizers of big agriculture. Natural sunshine, falling through smog-free skies, would grow them some food the way it was made to be grown. The climate was also perfect for growing marijuana – with hot, dry summers. A person could even make a living selling Humboldt pot – dozens of backwoods hippies were already doing it. Who knew they'd soon morph into a new hybrid, the Redneck Hippie, carrying guns, elaborately boobytrapping their pot patches, badmouthing newcomers and city-dwellers and generally exchanging pacifism, generosity and brotherly love for hypervigilant guardianship of their property and a deep distrust of strangers. They would become the types they had despised and rebelled against a few short years ago.

That summer, Tom and Rose had taken a trip to a tiny town west of Garberville, down a winding, potholed road and into the deep woods. They had seen a small, lopsided wood house for sale, close to the town's only store and post office, and had bought it immediately for a bargain price. There were acres of redwood forest, manzanita bushes, dry yellow weeds full of chirping crickets – there was even a tiny creek flowing, at least during the winter and spring months, out in the back of the house. There was a big clearing for a garden. This was the place, they thought, to settle down, raise some more kids and finally get away from the scary, hostile scene in the City, with its noise and traffic and hassle and perpetual cold fog and freaks everywhere just bringing you down.

Like thousands of peaceniks and flower children in big cities all over the country, they had had enough of the hostility, materialism and the violence which were infesting their neighborhood streets, enough of the cold concrete, the hookers and pimps and hustlers, and the heavy, hard-drug scene. San Francisco's rare warm days were gone for another year, and gone with them was the warm sense of community, friendship and love they had basked in for such a brief, precious time.

The easygoing dope smokers who used to dominate the streets were drifting away, going back to school so they could get a *real* job some day, going back to suburbia, with its room to spread out, grass to walk on, clean air and, yes, even its white picket fences. Some were going into politics – they were going to "change the system from within". Some were going back to the land – they were going to live the way their pioneer ancestors had: self-sufficient, strong and natural, in harmony with the Earth. Some were headed for Wall Street and some were headed for Silicon Valley.

The street was being filled by a hard-edged crowd who wanted a different kind of stimulation – the kind they got from methamphetamine – speed. Far from making people peaceful and friendly, speed fostered paranoia, hostility, anger and a cold-blooded greed unthinkable and intolerable to the pothead. The neighborhood became seedy, dangerous and cheap-looking almost overnight. They had come to San Francisco wearing flowers in their hair, just like the song said, and for a while, it had been enough. When it was Sunday afternoon and the street was swarming with beautiful, healthy young people, all rocking and rolling to a brand-new music, all bursting with love, all gazing blissfully through rose-colored glasses at the world in front of them and crazy to get to the fabulous future they would create, then San Francisco was the most fantastic place on Earth and they were the most fantastic generation ever born!

They would be the generation to put an end to war. Acceptance of the very idea of armed combat had to be changed into acceptance of, desire for, universal peace. Surely the mindless bloodbath of Vietnam, the thousands of body bags, the photos of burning villages and dead babies, the returning vets with their minds gone – surely these would make people see that war simply had to vanish from the human repertoire forever. The moms and dads weeping over flag-draped coffins simply could not fail to see, in the end, that their sons had died for nothing more noble than a standoff between two wrong ideologies, and served no good, greater or lesser.

They would be the generation to revolutionize the old, straightjacketed concepts of materialism and blind acquisition of wealth, of monogamy and possessiveness, of man's relation to and responsibility for his planet. They'd do it by shouting it out in the streets, if necessary. They would exploit the press they got for being dirty hippies by convincing the media to look beyond their long hair and their pot smoking and ask them about what they were *thinking. If only* they could convince the straight world to abandon the old, ineffectual and largely-unethical systems and change them for the better.

"I don't wanna raise our kids in this place," said Rose. "They're gonna make `em go to some overcrowded public school where they won't learn *any*thing about *real* life or the way things *should* be. Are they gonna teach them anything about waging peace? No. They're gonna teach them to get in line behind the soldiers marching off to war. Are they gonna teach them anything about giving? Or are they just gonna teach `em how to be good consumers – just how to *take*. And on and on. We can home-school the kids, if we have to. At least we can teach them how to be decent human beings, and not just taxpaying conformists!"

"Tell me about it," said Tom. He picked the baby up from the floor. "I can't remember a damn thing I supposedly learned in school, but I'm positive no teacher ever sat us down and told us anything about *life*. It was always just a bunch of names and dates you had to memorize – stuff that happened a thousand years ago – so you could pass the test the next day. I don't remember any tests to see if we knew how to change a tire or grow tomatoes or fix the pilot light on the stove or build a table.....stuff that might come in handy to know. They thought it was more important for us to know the exact date some document was signed than what the document actually *meant.* And if we didn't remember the exact date, we were failures, even if we understood the *concept* of the thing better than the teacher! Man," he said, brushing his hair out of his eyes and shifting the baby to the other hip, "I dunno. But we'll find some kind of alternative school up there – maybe we'll have to *start* one."

23 INTO THE SUNSET

Yesterday
Love was such an easy game to play
Now I need a place to hide away
Oh I believe in yesterday

Yesterday
Lennon/McCartney

Brandon and his brother sailed the boat from Sausalito to Honolulu in September of 1969. Carla took Darcy and got on an airplane for the first time in her life, landing in Honolulu two weeks before the brothers arrived. Meanwhile, she went to stay with Mack, an old friend of Brandon's who had also built his boat at the tannery. Mack took them in, but not for long. Women gave him the creeps, and kids were even worse. He drove down to the harbor and talked to David, who had sailed *Desperado* to Hawaii the year before. David had never met Carla, but felt any girlfriend of Brandon's had to be OK, and agreed to let them stay on his boat. Much relieved, Max delivered Carla and Darcy to the boat where it was moored along the harbor breakwater, introduced them, and sped away.

And a few nights later, when the moon was full and the clouds looked like soapsuds in blue-black water, when the soft, warm trade winds rustled the palm trees and the harbor lights glinted off the glossy waters, and the whole thing was like a postcard from Eden, Carla and David stepped into the old wooden dinghy, rowed slowly around the harbor, smoked a joint, gazed deeply into each others eyes and fell in lust.

They were under the influence. They were young and healthy. They were listening to the Beatles sing, *"Because the world is round, it turns me on....."* and they were duly turned on. The boat drifted gently, and they paddled it in a swirling circle and got dizzy. Their bloodstreams were flowing with hormones, Hawaiian grass and Primo Beer. Who knew that Free Love wasn't going to be so free anymore – that this time it was going to cost them. Brandon found out about the two of them almost as soon as he stepped off the boat. Carla found herself tearfully apologizing shortly thereafter, confessing to herself as much as to

Brandon that the affair was really one-sided.

"He doesn't want me," she said. "We're not going to run away together or anything like that. It was just sex."

But inside she was crushed by her own perception that David indeed did *not* want her. He liked her company, thought she was kinda cute, didn't mind the sex, but could have gotten that from any passing girl. He wasn't the pairing-off kind. He preferred the company of his boat-building buddies. Women, especially women with kids, eventually got in the way, started talking about living together and calling you their boyfriend and any number of intolerable, suffocating female traits. Sure, he wanted a woman *eventually*, but was holding out for a goddess worthy of his superior physical attributes and intellect. He was waiting for a woman who agreed with everything he said and did, someone who held as high an opinion of him as he did himself. And it wasn't Carla.

She found herself with a torch in her hand – a torch she would carry for much too long before reality finally blew it out. But while it still burned, she tortured David with proclamations of true love and cried several rivers over his unattainabliity and cool rejection. He made it clear enough in his noncommittal way, but she wouldn't see it. The oldest story in the world. She thought she would be in love with him forever, couldn't imagine ever feeling differently, couldn't believe he did not feel the same.

They stood on the deck of *Desperado*, docked in Sausalito, a year after she had gone back to the mainland with Brandon, after they had split up and after she and Blossom had become roommates in a tiny Noe Valley apartment in the City. She was wrapped against the harbor weather in her navy peacoat, and stood hiding under her hair and waiting for David's reply. It had been a simple question, requiring only a yes or no, but he had been thrown into a vat of mire by its implications.

He looked at his boots. He looked at the choppy gray water slapping the pilings. He looked at the very ends of the strands of blonde hair that flew away from Carla's shoulders - far away from her white face and green eyes. At last he turned sideways, then away, then looking back at her and tilting his head, he tried to smile but couldn't.

"I don't think so," he said.

He grabbed a handhold in the cockpit, ducked down, and went below. She heard the clinking noises of nautical hardware, the scuffling of boots, the low voices of David and Bob talking below.

She paused. She looked into the air and saw that everything had changed. Just like that. The sky around her, which had been merely blank and gray before, was now a hard steel blue, cold and sharp, and it was filled with the sounds of tearing chainsaws and driving, echoing hammers. The docks sloshed on a sewer of oily black water, clogged with beer cans and plastic diapers. Who *were* these assholes, she thought in a rage, who tossed their goddamn garbage in the ocean? She hated them. White fog poured like monster-movie smoke over the Sausalito hills, in from the scary, icy Pacific. She thought it couldn't possibly be any colder than this at the farthest end of the Earth.

Very slowly, very silently, she moved to the bow of the boat. She crouched down on the very tip of the fiberglass hull. He had of course made it smooth and white and flawless. Impenetrable. Beneath it, the water rocked and surged. She placed one foot, silent as a cat's paw, then the other, on the weather-silvered dock planks. For an instant, suspended, she listened. She heard the muffled movements and voices below and thought, without really thinking, that she'd never hear them again. Another instant, and her weight floated onto the dock and the boat slipped away. She almost ran down the dock, only wanting to get away without being seen, fearing the feeling of eyes on her back as she escaped. Her disappearance from his life had to be instant and unexpected and final. It was the only way.

Reaching the main road, she ran across to the gravel shoulder and turned to face oncoming traffic. She straightened, squinted into the afternoon light and stuck out her thumb. She remained rigid, with her face to the sharp wind, gulping back the ache rising in her throat. For the thousandth time, she wished she could take it all back. Every word, every action, *everything.*

A big, lumbering stepvan pulled over, sending chunks of grit flying into her eyes. Glad to find shelter, desperate to get away from here and home and curled into the blankets of her little bed in San Francisco, she quickly climbed up into the cab, where two longhaired guys greeted her with broad grins. As she pulled the door closed, she saw David's car turn onto the shoulder of the road just in front of the truck. She stared. She could see him looking back at her in the rearview mirror.

The driver of the van took in the situation immediately. He held up his hands and smiled at her.

"Do you want a ride, or what?"

"Yeah! Thanks. Yeah. Let's get outta here."

"Well, alright!" he laughed, and put the van in gear.

She turned to accept the joint being handed to her by a sleepy-eyed guy crouched between the two seats, and kept her head turned in his direction, taking a big drag, as they passed David's car and headed out of town.

The sun was lowering beyond the Gate and they drove into the tunnel between Sausalito and the bridge. Carla looked at the rainbow painted around the tunnel entrance with dead eyes. It was faded and filthy and its colors seemed a ridiculous, false version of actual, hopeful hues. The guy crouching next to her took a big drag from the roach on his feathered alligator clip and beamed at her with heavy-lidded eyes and a beatific grin.

"Don't even think about it," she said, and grabbed the clip.

EPILOGUE
A LONG TIME GONE

"We are here to make a better world. No amount of rationalization or blaming can preempt the moment of choice each of us brings to our situation here on this planet. The lesson of the 60's is that people who cared enough to do right could change history. We didn't end racism but we ended legal segregation. We ended the idea that you could send half-a-million soldiers around the world to fight a war that people do not support. We ended the idea that women are second-class citizens. We made the environment an issue that couldn't be avoided. The big battles that we won cannot be reversed. We were young, self-righteous, reckless, hypocritical, brave, silly, headstrong and scared half to death. And we were right."

Abbie Hoffman

And I don't know a soul who's not been battered, don't have a friend who feels at ease
Don't know a dream that's not been shattered or driven to its knees

But it's alright, it's alright, for we lived so well, so long Still, when I think of the road we're traveling on I wonder what's gone wrong
I can't help it.....I wonder what's gone wrong

American Tune
Paul Simon

We wanted to make a better world because we found it lacking. It lacked humanity and honesty and peace and selflessness. We knew that the very worst problem in the world wasn't communism or atheism or disrespect for a piece of cloth on a pole. No communist had ever taken away our freedom of speech – that was done to us by our own government, our own countrymen, our parents and even our peers. No atheist had ever burned a cross on anyone's lawn or bombed an abortion clinic – that was done by the self-described devout followers of Christ next door. They were doing the work their omnipotent god somehow wasn't able to do himself. These were the people who would tell you in one breath that mere mortals were incapable of understanding God's "mysterious ways", and in the next, that they knew *exactly* what God wanted

288

us to do. He wanted us to worship him and stop killing embryos. Because killing is wrong. And the appropriate punishment for killing someone is *being killed* by someone else.

No flag or American birth certificate had ever protected us from being gunned down in the street by the cops and the National Guard – we found we had to try and protect ourselves and each other from the *real, immediate* enemy within our own borders. The worst problems in the world for us were domestic: home-grown prejudice, greed, dishonesty, racial and sexual inequality, hypocrisy, homophobia and violence. Hadn't we paid attention when our parents and teachers told us these were bad human traits and that we should not practice them? Didn't they teach us to share? Didn't they teach us to always tell the truth, and to be nice to everyone, regardless of physical appearance, to never point and stare, never call people names and to never, *ever* hit each other? These admonishments had the ring of truth, because they corresponded to what we instinctively felt inside when we chose right over wrong. It was called a conscience, and it used to seem innate.

We wanted to make a better America for the very reason that so many people *did not.* There were a lot of us, but we were a small minority in comparison with the millions whose concept of this country was that it was, always had been and always would be the greatest nation the world had ever known, and it *did not need improvement.* Furthermore, anyone who suggested that any part of it needed fixing was nothing less than a traitor who deserved to be shot.

We were confronted with the right-wing slogan, "My country, right or wrong". We unapologetically perceived the glaring hypocrisy embedded in that kind of jingoistic non-logic, and we categorically rejected the whole idea of supporting any idea or any action which was *wrong.* This kind of thinking, that America could do what she would and we had no right to examine or criticize, was a little too reminiscent of historically-recent totalitarian ideologies from both ends of the political spectrum. Citizens of Nazi Germany were not allowed to criticize their government any more than were the citizens of the Soviet Union, and we took such tremendous national pride in *not being like them.* Our national anthem reminded us, at every ballgame, that we were living in the "land of the free", and our most fundamental freedom was the freedom of speech – the very right straight America wanted to take away from us, while retaining it for themselves. When we saw the hypocrisy of our countrymen not following their own rules, we rebelled.

We left home – left the security and predictability which conformity would have guaranteed – and struck out on our own to see if we could find others who shared our ideas and ideals. We found them in numbers we hadn't even been allowed to imagine; our parents and teachers had assured us individually that we were ridiculous and crazy and therefore alone in the world, that we needed psychiatric help or a good beating with a belt, or both, that we needed to just do what they ordered us to do and shut our ungrateful mouths, because soldiers were dying for our right to *open* our ungrateful mouths.

Our parents and teachers could like it or not – we were *not* alone and we were going to change the world *together.*

If racism still exists, it's not because we did not try to end it. If one man still hates another because of the color of his skin, it's because he never recognized his hatred as an undesirable human trait, never admitted a need to change himself, never took responsibility for his own behavior – it's because he is morally lazy. If we had been able to force him to change his very *thoughts*, we would have. But we couldn't, so we had to use the law to prevent him from *acting* on those thoughts.

We didn't end the idea of fighting unpopular wars on anything but a temporary basis. Although we may very well have been the force that finally brought the troops home from Vietnam (and that opinion will vary, depending on whom you ask), we've lived long enough to see history repeat itself in Afghanistan and Iraq. This time, it seems our collective will to prevent it had flown south to its Palm Beach vacation home, and our will to stop it, once it had begun, had dried up along with our hormones. We were more inclined, as a group, to sit this one out because we've grown accustomed to our affluence and our comfort, grown used to the idea of neverending war as a fact of life, and we're just plain tired. We needed the politicized students, the young and energetic, to take up the torch and carry it forward. But though millions marched, the Masters of the Universe remained immune and exempt and the button was pushed. Again.

Women are still second-class citizens. Men will never completely relinquish their self-appointed dominance, even if it's just by a fraction of an inch, even if they have to take Viagra to artificially maintain it. Check the statistics. Women still make less money for the same work. A lot of Baby Boomers are still alive, and we grew up with the ethos and mores of our parents, which they got from *their* parents. We perceived a lot of their examples as lessons on how *not* to behave, and one of those, for a lot of females anyway, was that we were not born subservient. We had value beyond that of sexual receptacle, cook and baby factory, and had our own intellect, creativity and ability which were every bit as legitimate as any man's. But a lot of men were far too comfortable with the concept of domination over the "weaker" sex, and only managed a thinly-veiled pretense of gender equality long enough to get what they wanted in the first place.

We brought up the subject of the environment 50 years ago. We saw slow death coming down the road. We did the math – finite resources plus infinite population equals crisis. We started recycling. We grew our own. We went organic. We hugged trees and saved the whales. We embraced birth control and communal living and alternative energy. We thought it would catch on, people would wise up and things would change. The only thing that changed was the rate at which the planet is suffocating. Since it's a basic human trait to wait until a catastrophic event occurs before becoming concerned, since we're not inclined towards prevention, only towards the application of tiny bandaids after the patient has bled to death, we may not have the ability to get ourselves out of the situations we've created and continue to create. In spite of the mountains of evidence which chronicle our arrogant disregard for the health of the planet and the murder/suicide pact we're engaged in, our governments continue to make the least correct, most damaging choices at every opportunity, choices which benefit the few in the short term at the expense of the many in the long term. History simply doesn't have the power to teach someone who doesn't see a need to learn. And when it comes to the point where people start denying scientific fact in favor of religious mythology and partisan entrenchment, it gets scary for the sane ones.

The big battles that we won apparently *can* be reversed. The Patriot Act is a concept straight from the pages of *1984* and the minds which conceived it and allowed its continued existence and application are the minds which would gladly reverse every righteous victory ever won. Freedom of speech and expression, of the press and of religion – our basic birthrights – *can* be taken away from us – not by "communists" or "terrorists" or by shadowy, foreign figures seeking to destroy our sacred American way of life, but by our next-door neighbors who are more than willing to shed blood, *our* blood, to prevent us from changing their *personal* American Way of Life, which very closely resembles nothing so much as blind acquisition and one-upmanship. They would gleefully strip the rest of us of all freedom if, in doing so, they could guarantee their favored status on the wealth/power continuum.

So in some ways, our ideals would always be just that. Pipe dreams. Utopian wish-lists. There has never been a time and never will be a time when all humans will live together in peace. No, Rodney. We can *not* all just get along.

Paul Simon's masterpiece, American Tune, seems to be a requiem for our very *will* to do right. The slow demise of our passion and hope began with the shock of realization that our government lies to us and hides information from us to keep us controlled and dependent, that war as a human endeavor will never end and that money actually *does* buy happiness. When he says, "We lived so well so long", he's not talking about our standard of living as much as about our standards *for* living. The affluence and prosperity and optimism we enjoyed in our childhood were tied to and dependent upon our ethics and priorities as a nation. Peace wasn't just a word or a romantic ideal to those who had lived through two World Wars – it was absolutely necessary to the quality of life everyone thought they had earned at last. We had our hearts broken by the reality of another invented war, and then another. We let our lack of a voice be heard to try and prevent it, and when that was predictably brushed off by not only the war creators but by the mothers and fathers of soon-to-be-dead soldiers, we did what we were compelled to do. We protested against it *again.*

America is like a junkie who never went into rehab but never died, either. She just goes on and on, eating more than she needs, buying more than she wants, mindlessly competitive, mindlessly aggressive, concerning herself with nothing beyond the boundaries of her own self-promotion, ignorant and proud of it, disregarding and denying anything that doesn't serve her habit, amoral, blind and going backwards in time. What's gone wrong is we've forgotten, if we ever knew, the difference between a technical, legal right and moral correctness. Americans feel they have the right to do anything they want, conveniently leaving out the other half of the sentence: "as long as it doesn't harm anyone else." A crucial omission, and at the bottom of every problem and struggle and conflict. Our egocentricity – the idea that one man can afford to exclude all others, that one nation can afford to dismiss all others, that our lifestyle, religion and political systems are the apex of human achievement and philosophy, sacred and unimpeachable, eternal and unchanging – this hubris has conceived, designed, excavated, paved and painted the white stripe down the middle of the "road we're traveling on".

But we're dreamers. We were born to want to travel on the very best road we can conceive in our free, brave dreams, and if the old road isn't good enough, to tear it up and build a new one.